# HAIR POWER

# PIERS ANTHONY

**Hair Power**
Copyright © 2016 by Piers Anthony

**Cover Art**
Mac Hernandez
**Editor-in-Chief**
Kristi King-Morgan
**Formatting**
Niki Browning

Printed in the United States of America

First Printing, 2016

ISBN 13: 978-1534919143
ISBN 10: 1534919147

Dreaming Big Publications

www.dreamingbigpublications.com

# CONTENTS

# CHAPTER 1:
## *Hairball*

Quiti was no quitter, but she was looking for a place to quit. It was a beautiful Sunday morning, a really lovely sunny day, but it was wasted on her. She walked past City Hall, which was close to her home; it was a small town. She admired its classic architecture, but this too was largely wasted on her. She paused to study herself in the reflection of a dirty deserted store window; the recession had been bad for local business. She looked like an ill mannequin, with her bald head and pudgy face, and felt worse. Her nausea was not merely from the fading remnant of the last chemo treatment, but from her realistic assessment of her prospects.

"As with Rome in the late days," she murmured. "Before she mends, must sicken worse."

Except that she would not mend. Her parents were in denial, her doctors were locked into fake smiles, her friends were avoiding the subject, but she knew the truth: Her condition was terminal. Already she felt the dread cancer pushing at her brain, trying to assume complete possession of the remaining space within her skull. She needed constantly stronger doses of pain medication. The chemo was supposed to extend her survival as much as six months, but she knew that was hopelessly optimistic.

Why wait for the visions fostered by the potent treatments, the hallucinations, the loss of her besieged sense of self as the monster inside her head consumed her identity? Better, far better, to deal with it early, before she became a mere parody of what was once an ordinary college age girl? To end it in her own fashion, by her own decision, cleanly, efficiently. She had the sharp paring knife; one firm slash across her throat would delete her consciousness and allow her to bleed out painlessly before anyone found her. All she needed was a sufficiently private place, and a bit of deadly courage.

Which was why she was here in the derelict section of town. A deserted warehouse seemed ideal. It might be days before anyone checked it. She had written her farewell note and left it under her pillow where it would be found when they searched her room for clues to her disappearance. The note thanked her folks for their patience and support, said she loved them, and regretted the pain she had caused them. "It wasn't anyone's fault," it concluded. "Maybe I will see you again in Heaven." She didn't believe in Heaven or in any afterlife, but they did, so that might be some scant comfort to them.

She continued walking, approaching a large silent building. Its wide double doors were locked, but there might be an entrance via the small office section. A boy she knew had mentioned how he and his friends sneaked in to smoke pot in private. So there was a way. All she had to do was find it.

The office door was latched but not locked. She entered cautiously, just in case there was an employee or a security guard; she didn't want to have to try to explain her business there. There was no one. Behind the desk, at the rear, was an inner door marked EMPLOYEES ONLY. This too was unlocked.

She entered that barn-like main warehouse. It was hot

and gloomy. Perfect!

*Please.*

Quiti paused. Had someone spoken to her? All she saw was a yard-wide clump of fur on the barren floor, or maybe a giant hairball. Had her slightly guilty conscience addressed her, trying to dissuade her from her purpose? "Is someone here?" she asked.

*Please. Help me.*

Quiti focused on the hairball. "Is that you?" she asked.

*Please. I am in pain. I need light.*

It was definitely the hairball, and it was evidently telepathic. Was she having a hallucination already? Well, maybe even that deserved some respect. "Who are you?"

*Call me Hair Brain. Who are you?*

Fair enough; it seemed that her limited imagination had some humor. Hair brain, rather than hare brain. "Hello, Hair Brain. I am Quiteria, Quiti for short. I am a twenty year old nondescript human female."

*May I explore your mind, Quiti?*

Why the hell not? It wasn't as if any of this came from anywhere outside her sick head. "Go ahead, if it doesn't take too long."

*It is instant. I have done it. I like you, Quiti. You have sterling qualities of character.*

As if her own hallucination was going to dislike her? Maybe it feared she would banish it if it didn't flatter her. "How can I help you, Hair Brain?"

*I need light to feed on. I am alien to this world. I hid here to avoid awkward discovery and got trapped. Please.*

That was straightforward. "You are a visitor from another planet?"

*I am.*

She wasn't sure she believed that, but again there was the matter of respect. "You mean no harm to the folk of this world?"

*No harm. I am here to recruit emissaries to facilitate diplomatic communication between our worlds.*

If this stemmed from her own fevered imagination, she had more wit than she thought, being a grade C student and person throughout her young life. Determination and realism were most of what little she had going for her. Maybe she was adapting from some cheap sci-fi effort she had seen in passing and forgotten. "You need light. Will sunlight do?"

*Yes!*

She approached the hairball. From up close she saw that the hair radiated out from a smaller center, maybe like a sea anemone. It probably did not weigh much. "I will pick you up and take you outside, into the sunlight. Will that do?"

*Yes.*

On any other occasion she might have been concerned about touching such a weird hairy thing. But what did it matter? It was a construct of her ill imagination, and in any event she would soon be dead. "I must put my hands on you. Please don't sting me, or whatever it is you do."

*No sting*, it agreed.

She squatted, reaching to the base of the thing. She touched it with her fingers, and it did not sting her. She cupped her two hands and heaved it up. It weighed about twenty pounds; she could handle it. Its radiating hair was in her face, but she could see though to the doorway beyond. She walked carefully to that doorway, made her way through the small office, and on outside into the sunlight.

*Light!* The thought was phenomenally gratified. She could feel the delight in the creature.

She set the hairball down on a chest-high loading dock outside the building and stepped back. "There you are, alien envoy. Do you need anything else?"

Hair Brain fluffed out its hair, becoming significantly larger. It rose off the dock, and settled down again. Its color shifted, becoming scintillating. The direct sunlight was doing it worlds of good. *Yes. I need to repay your kindness, Quiti. What can I do for you in return for saving me?*

She shook her head. What could a fantasy image do for her, really? "There is no need. I'm just glad to have helped."

*I insist. I must do you an equivalent return favor.*

Too bad this wasn't real! She could have asked for a cure for her cancer. Now she just needed to wrap this up so she could get on with her real business here, before she lost her nerve. So she made a facetious request. "How about a really nice head of hair, so I won't be bald anymore?"

*Excellent choice. Do not move.*

Then the hair ball floated off the dock, came toward her, and landed on her bald head. Astonished, she stood perfectly still. It felt like a heavy helmet. Her skin tingled where it touched, not unpleasantly. Something was happening.

Then it lifted off and returned to the dock. *It will grow soon.*

"Uh, thank you," she said. "Now if that's all, I will leave you."

*Until we meet again.* Then the hair ball faded out.

The hallucination was over, but her head still tingled. Almost as if the incident had been real.

Quiti faced the office. But something stopped her. Her suicidal depression was gone. She no longer wanted to kill herself. Her reasons remained, but it was clear she was not up to doing it today.

What could she do? She shrugged and walked back toward home.

# CHAPTER 2:
## *Wig*

Quiti's home was her parents' small house in a suburb of the town, neatly kept but nondescript. They were an absolutely ordinary family of three. Her father, Bill, worked in a furniture company office, earning enough but not more than enough to make the mortgage payments and basic expenses. He might have gotten a promotion, but had turned it down. Why? Because he needed to stay where he was, within walking distance of his job, with the insurance he had, to support his ill daughter. Quiti hated that, but could not deny its validity; she needed to remain where she was too, with the hospital close and support available for her condition. That guilt was part of what had caused her to make the decision to kill herself. Her folks needed to be free of the burden of her.

So what had changed? Because she no longer had any intention of dying. Not today, not tomorrow, not in six months, in fact not ever. She had become excruciatingly positive in the last hour, and knew it would not abate. Because of her encounter with the hairball.

It stemmed from the bald skin of her head. Something was there that radiated a positive mood, senseless as that might seem. Maybe she had imagined the whole sequence, yet her outlook had suffered a change. *She was not going to die.*

How could she know that? Logically, it was nonsensical. Had she joined her parents in delusion? "Denial: it's not just a river in Africa," she muttered, repeating a saying she had heard when talking with other cancer patients. They, too, had families and friends who could not accept the reality of their conditions, and it was cruel to try to argue with them. What would be, would be, regardless of what they chose to believe. That applied especially to her parents, who simply could not accept the loss of their child, however ordinary she might be.

Quiti had always been a grade C student, safely above failing, but also safely below any possible academic ambition. She was in college because of a class-action grant that applied to students like her, intended to provide them some distraction while nature took its inevitable course. Her grades hardly mattered, since she would never have the chance to make effective use of what she learned. The other students were familiar with her situation, and recognized her, either bald or with her cheap wig. They never teased her. Not since the diagnosis. That, actually, was disquieting; it meant they were indulging in a grim deathwatch.

And of course she had no boyfriend. She would have welcomed one, and probably would have given him anything he wanted, just to maintain the relationship. It wasn't cancer that was responsible, it was that she was totally plain. Her face was on the negative side of ordinary, with a nose slightly big, mouth slightly irregular, and her body had always been slightly chubby. Boys simply were not turned on, even those whose horizons were limited to thoughtless sex. She was not appealing even as a one night stand.

She entered the house. Her mother, Betty, was there in a moment. "Quiti! Where were you? I worried."

"I took a walk, Mom. Just sorting out my feelings."

"You must have good feelings! They are too negative at the hospital; I know you will recover."

"Yes I will," Quiti agreed. Now, oddly, she believed it.

"Lunch will be ready soon, dear. You must eat well."

Suddenly Quiti was ravenously hungry. That was odd, as her appetite had been at best indifferent, thanks in part to the sieges of nausea. But she had no nausea now. "I will eat very well," she agreed.

Her mother bustled off to the kitchen, thrilled by Quiti's promise to have appetite. Betty could have taken an odd job to assist the family's finances but that prospect had faded with the illness. Now she had to be constantly at home, to take care of Quiti in case she had an emergency. This was not unrealistic; sometimes Quiti suffered severe dizziness, and might fall and hurt herself. She felt guilty for that, too.

She went to her bedroom. The first thing she did was remove the suicide note from under the pillow; it was no longer applicable. The second thing was to strip naked and gaze at herself in the long mirror.

She was simply not impressive, quite apart from her baldness. She stood five and a half feet tall, her posture was a slouch, her belly protruded, and the fat on her buttocks was flabby rather than sexy. Her breasts were simply additional lumps of slightly sagging fat rather than beacons of feminine appeal. She couldn't blame the boys; if she were male, she would not be interested in a body like this either.

She straightened up and inhaled. All that happened was that the lumps of fat became more prominent, while her belly barely tightened.

So why the hell was she so positive? This was a hundred and eighty degrees contrary to reality.

She sighed and put on a dress. Then she donned her wig. It was a motley brown affair, second hand from a girl who no longer lived. It did improve her appearance somewhat, if only because it hid her baldness and framed her face so that her pimples no longer showed.

She went down to lunch. Betty had made egg salad

sandwiches. They were delicious. Quiti gulped them down so fast that her mother was astonished. "Great, mom! I'm still hungry."

Her mother plainly did not know what to make of this change. "I have leftovers, but—"

"I'll take them!"

She did, and soon her belly was full. Sometimes the act of eating had stirred up her digestive system, so that she had had to chew and swallow slowly lest she vomit the meal back out. But she was full and fine now.

Could an imaginary hairball alien have accomplished this? It did not seem likely. But then, what *did* account for it?

After lunch Quiti returned to her room, brushed her teeth, and did an impromptu dance as if she were happy. How could she be happy? Was she absolutely crazy? Was her hallucination the first sign of her burgeoning insanity, as the tumors shoved at her brain?

Somehow it did not seem so. She had no headache, no dizziness, no discomfort whatsoever. She did not need a pain pill. She felt better than she had in months.

Well, she could check to see whether she was really in good shape. She lay on her bed and did leg lifts, which normally wore her out after a few repetitions. They were fine. She did sit ups, and they were fine. She got on the floor and did push-ups, and they too were fine. Finally she went to the clothing bar in her closet and did a pull-up. Normally that would poop her out entirely; she simply did not have the muscle.

She did three pull-ups and paused, breathing hard. Was this possible? Her record, set before the illness, was five. So she did three more.

This was weird. She did not have the muscle. Was she just imagining it? That seemed more likely. First the hairball, then the fitness. Imagination was cheap.

She lay on the bed and pondered. She needed to get a

grasp on reality, and for that she needed help

Well, she would get it. Decisions were coming more readily now. In fact her mind felt uncommonly clear.

She clapped the wig back on her head. "I'm going out for another walk," she called to her mother as she left the house.

The moment she was out in the sunlight, her scalp itched. She pulled off the wig so that the rays struck her skin. Then her head felt wonderful.

"The hair," she murmured. "Hair Brain gave me hair. It must need the sun, just as he does." The hairball had become male in her mind, for convenience. "So forget the wig; soak my head in sun."

There was a small community playground two blocks distant from the house. She walked there. Three teen boys were playing bat and fetch with a softball. She knew them; in the old days she had joined them in such exercises, though she had never been very good at them.

They spied her. "Hi, Quiti!" one called. Not Baldy, Girly, or any other derisive name, and no razzing; as with the others, they knew. It was a neighborhood conspiracy. Their special politeness covered their pity. "Wanna take a bat?"

Actually, yes, now that she thought of it. That should quickly show her physical reality. "Sure, Speedo."

She took her place at bat. Speedo was pitcher, with the second boy playing catcher and the third in the field, not far out. He sent an underhand pitch, not at all as hard as he could; she was after all a sick girl.

She swung, connected, and hit the ball out over the fielder's head.

All three boys stood still, staring at her. "You on steroids, girl?" Speedo asked.

"I don't think so. But there's no telling what meds they put me on. I just felt strong, and thought it was imaginary. That hit must have been a fluke; you know I'm not that

9

good."

Of course they knew, and did not say. "Wanna try it again?"

"Yes, if it's okay with you. I don't want to mess up your game."

The boys laughed good-naturedly. "It's just practice," Speedo said as he recovered the ball.

He pitched again, this time lower and faster. She swung again, connected, and again the ball sailed well out into the field. This time the fielder was out there, and chased it, but it was still beyond him.

Quiti shook her head. "I can't explain it. Usually I'm lucky just to hit the ball, and it goes about ten feet. Something's making me feel strong. Maybe it *is* the meds." Though she was not on any meds at the moment.

Speedo considered. "Wanna arm wrestle?"

And he had real muscles in his arms. But it might be a valid test. "Go easy on me," she said. "I'm *really* no good at this."

They went to a park bench and set up for a contest, hands linked, elbows on the table. "Starting," Speedo said, and applied slow pressure.

Quiti returned it. He pushed harder. She pushed back harder. He applied real force. She resisted, but was slowly being overwhelmed. So there were limits to this mysterious power. "You got me," she said.

He stopped immediately. "But you're pretty strong."

She laughed. "For a sick girl."

"For anyone."

"I'll have to go ask what's in those meds."

"Can you get some for us?"

She shook her head. "It's probably illegal, outside the lab."

"You wanna join our team?"

"No way. When this stuff wears off, I'll be nothing

again. But thanks for humoring me."

"You're more of a woman than I took you for, Quiti. If I were your age, I'd ask you for a date."

"Fortunately you aren't. You won't need to embarrass yourself with a bald girl."

"You got a wig, don't you?"

She produced her wig. "Yes. But all it does is make me a nothing in a wig."

"I'm not sure of that." This was a more thoughtful boy than she had supposed. She had evidently won his respect by showing some physical prowess, and he wasn't concerned about her dull appearance. "I think you're pretty good to handle your condition the way you do. I'd have freaked out."

Was this getting serious? Would she consider going out with a sixteen year old boy? "Thanks, no thanks. You are kind to offer, but I have to get home."

"If you change your mind—"

"I'll let you know." She walked away.

Now she had at least two things to ponder. It seemed that her new-found strength was real, and she might actually get a date, at least for a day. Would she care to make out with an underage boy? That could be legal trouble. But he would never tell where it counted.

That evening she went for her college math class. She was abysmal in math, but she liked the people in it, so she normally suffered though. She had donned her wig, as the professor felt that it was less distracting to others than her bald head. This time her scalp did not tingle, maybe because there was no sunlight to be had.

She was early. So was her friend Kate, who had been treated for skin cancer and survived, so she understood about chemo and nausea. "I couldn't make head or tail of the assignment," Kate confided. "This calculus—it makes no sense to me."

"It does make sense," Quiti said. "Ordinary math can't

properly handle things like trajectories or gravitational attraction, which have changing ratios, but calculus can. So if you want to be an astronaut, it's better to know it."

"Quiti! You actually sound as if you understand it!"

"Well, it's not that complicated when you get into it. You just have to understand its basis, starting with derivatives. They're not Greek even if some Greek symbols are used."

"But this example in the book—that sure is Greek to me!"

"No, no. That's just the rationale for calculating a graph or chart that is logarithmic in nature. It's simple, really." She went on to clarify it for her friend.

"I'll be damned," Kate said. "It does make sense! Thank you, thank you!"

"Max the exam," Quiti said.

"And why didn't you max it?" a voice behind her asked.

Quiti jumped. It was Professor Taylor, the math teacher! He had come in while she was distracted clarifying the example for Kate. "I'm sorry," Quiti said. "I didn't mean to interrupt the class."

"You flunked that example yourself," Taylor said. "But obviously you understand it very well. What happened?"

What had happened, indeed! Quiti suddenly realized that she had not just gained physical strength today, she had become far more intelligent. She understood things she had never grasped before. How could that be? This was distinctly weird. But she needed an answer for the moment, so she tried to make a joke of it. "Today I have my thinking cap on." She touched her wig.

The professor laughed. "That must be it. Keep it on." He moved on to start the class. But she knew he would not be forgetting this incident.

Quiti was increasingly certain that her encounter with the hairball had not been a hallucination. Hair Brain had given her something that was changing her life. How and why were things she would still have to figure out.

When she got home that evening and gazed at herself in the mirror, she discovered that her head was no longer quite bald. It was covered with a mat of very short hair, like five o'clock shadow on a man.

She was actually growing a new head of hair. But she strongly suspected that that was the least of it.

# CHAPTER 3:
## *Date*

In the next ten days her hair grew to an inch in length. She went out daily to walk in the sun, because the hair was hungry for energy. It was translucent to the point of invisibility, but when she focused, it could change color, becoming brown, blond, red, black, gray, or actually any color at all, including blue, green, or even striped or polka dotted. Yet she had the feeling that this was only the beginning of its properties.

She ate voraciously, everything her mother provided and more. She also went quietly out back and scooped up handfuls of dirt, swallowing them. She knew this was for the hair: it needed more than a standard diet provided. She obliged it without telling her folks, knowing that they would think her crazy. The hairball had certainly come through for her in that respect: she now had hair like no other. Yet despite her huge intake, she was losing weight. Her face and body were becoming lean. She had to eat even more. How could she do it without attracting unwanted attention?

Maybe there was a way. She walked to Speedo's house. "I need a favor," she told him. "I need to eat a lot without other folk knowing. Could you take me to an all you can eat place and pretend you're eating most of it? I'll pay for it. I just need privacy."

"Sure," he said eagerly. "Anything you want, Quiti."

"What can I do for you in return?"

He gazed at her, and she knew he was seeing what she couldn't conceal: she was no longer chubby or pimply. She was a lean mean machine. Some of it was improved posture, but more was robustly improving fitness. Her legs were muscling out, her waist was thinning, and her perky breasts now rested upon a nicely contoured chest. Only her still seemingly bald head marred the effect. She had become sexy.

"Not that favor," she said before he spoke. "It's not that you are unworthy or unattractive, Speedo. It's that I am twenty and you are sixteen. It would be statutory rape on my part. I have problems enough without getting mired in that sort of hassle. Otherwise I would do it."

"I wouldn't tell."

"You're a virile young man. You'd have to tell. Otherwise it wouldn't count."

He did not argue the case. "Damn. And I'll bet you could beat me now at arm wrestling."

"Speedo, I'm not here to embarrass you."

"But you could. You're just bursting with vigor. It's not just sex appeal."

She nodded. "Ask for something else."

"Well, there's a dance tomorrow, and I don't have a date," he said hesitantly. "You—you weren't much, before, but now you're a bombshell."

"Thank you. That I can do. I will be your girl for the dance. I will dress pretty, I will kiss you, I will put on the show. Everyone will know you have a viable companion."

"Great! It's a date."

"It's a date," she agreed. "I'll even put on a more attractive wig."

"Yeah." He was understandably at a loss to say more about that.

Then she thought of something else. Not only was he

believing her, he was pretty sharp. She could use his active support. "Speedo, can I trust you?"

"Quiti, I can't help looking!"

He had misunderstood. "You may look," she agreed, opening her blouse so that he could see down into her vibrant bosom. "This is something else."

He licked his lips. "Anything!"

"It's that I have hair now, but I don't want others to know. Will you help me keep that secret?"

"Sure!"

"Like this." She focused, and turned her hair brown. "Wow!"

Then she turned it blue.

"Don't do that in public!" he said, alarmed.

"But if I forget, and it shows a color, you'll help cover for me."

"Oh, yes! How do you do it?"

"That's a story. I'll tell you, if."

"I don't have to talk about that. I won't tell."

"Thank you. Now let's go and gorge." She handed him a twenty dollar bill. "You'll pay."

"Quiti, you don't need to—"

"Humor me. And cover for me. Here and at the dance."

"Okay!"

They walked to Joe's All You Can Eatery, where a single cover charge per person sufficed. They loaded their plates high and went to a booth, where Speedo nibbled and Quiti ate ninety percent of both plates. Then they refilled them and continued.

"Wow," Speedo murmured. "You weren't kidding about eating a lot."

"We can go slower for dessert. Then I'll talk."

The proprietor, Joe, had kept on eye on them, to make sure the food wasn't being wasted. "I've got half a left over wedding cake in back I need to use up. You want it?"

"Oh, yes," Quiti agreed.

They took the huge portion and she dug in. Between mouthfuls she spoke. "You can believe me or not. Just don't tell."

"Got it."

"I was going to kill myself, since I'll soon be dying in pain anyway. You know, cut to the chase."

"Don't do it, Quiti!"

"Instead I met this alien telepathic hairball trapped in a warehouse. I helped him get into the sunlight, and he floated up and sat on my head to give me a nice head of hair. Now I'm spending a lot of time in the sun, and eating a lot, to give the hair energy and substance. It's some hair."

"It sure is! But it doesn't make sense."

She shrugged. "I said you don't have to believe."

"I believe! I have a feel for aliens. I love ET type movies. But why didn't the hairball float up out of there on his own? He didn't need you to let him out."

"Well, the door was latched."

"He could have pushed the latch himself. Quiti, that wasn't chance. He was waiting for you."

She stared at him. "Why?"

"Because maybe the kind of help he needed wasn't getting out of a warehouse. Maybe it was a good person with nothing to lose. For something bigger than just hair."

It was a revelation. Of course it was true! "He did say we would meet again. I didn't credit it because I didn't figure to be alive that long."

"He read your mind. He knew you were a good person. Quiti, I think he gave you more than hair."

"Hair like this isn't enough?"

"What good would a dead girl be to him? That hair is giving you health."

"It certainly is. It's making me strong and smart, and I think it's starting to make me telepathic." She was saying too much, but she was tuning in to his mind and knew she could trust him. It was a relief to have such a dialogue at last.

"And I'll bet it's curing your cancer."

She stared again. "My cancer!"

He nodded. "I think you owe that alien."

"Oh my god," she breathed. Then she leaned forward and kissed him on the mouth.

"I want to be your friend," he said, pleased. "Even if it's without benefits. I think you have much more of a future than you expected."

Her head was spinning, and not from illness. "Yes to both, I think."

It was time to move on. Her belly was so full it almost looked as if she were pregnant, but she felt comfortable and exhilarated.

"About the dance," she said. "I really don't want to advertise how I've changed, especially if I'm going to be around for the long haul. Is it okay with you if I'm anonymous? Like a masked visitor?"

"Great!"

Next evening they went to the dance. Her belly was already flat; her digestion had improved significantly along with the rest of her. She wore a flaring skirt and tight blouse, and her new wig was glorious. The mask covered only her eyes, really concealing nothing, but her face had changed enough so that it was unlikely that anyone would recognize her. Certainly her body was from another realm. She took Speedo's arm as they entered the chamber, and she knew that all eyes were upon them. She smiled and inhaled, knowing that she threatened to burst out of the blouse. She was giving them the show, making the boys envy Speedo.

They registered at the desk. "Speedo," he said. "And my date, the visiting Lady Excelsior." He paid the fee and filled out the name tags.

They danced. She whirled, making her skirt spread out

in a full circle, showing off her legs. After the first dance, the men started cutting in. She accommodated them, she now had coordination beyond her fondest prior ambitions, and was mistress of all the intricate steps. Speedo plainly didn't mind; a date like this added significantly to his teen credits. Between dances she was with him, smiling and giving him her full rapt attention. She was really enjoying the script, which was totally alien (no pun) to her prior existence.

"Who *are* you?" one man asked. "I know all the gals around here, but I don't know you."

Because he had paid no attention to the sick chubby girl no one wanted to date. But she knew him: a handsome rake. But, true to her identity as a visitor, she merely smiled. "You would not believe my origin, stranger."

"Come have a drink with me."

She glanced around and saw that Speedo was dancing with a pretty girl. He was evidently more in demand now that he had proven his mettle by snagging a beauteous visitor. "One," she agreed. "Then I must return to my date."

They went to the bar where he ordered mellow vodka. Vodka was notorious for its deceptive mildness that masked a hundred proof alcohol or more; it was possible to get drunk before one realized. But she could handle alcohol; she had tried it privately, making sure. She could not get drunk; the energy went straight to feed the hair.

She knew with the first sip that the drink was spiked. Probably the date rape drug. But she also felt her system marshaling to counter it. That was a new talent of the hair, somehow protecting her internally as well as externally, and not just from alcohol. She continued drinking, tuning in on the man's mood: he was hot for sex. As if she needed even token telepathy to pick up on that.

"Thank you," she said as she finished. "It's a very nice drink." Then she returned to Speedo, who of course was not drinking, being underage. That was just as well.

Immediately another man came to their table. "I hear you're good with cars," he said to Speedo. "I got engine trouble, and I have to make a rendezvous. Can you help?"

Speedo glanced at Quiti. "Go ahead," she said. "I'll keep."

He got up and accompanied the man outside. Whereupon the rake moved in. So it was a setup to get her alone. This was interesting.

"How you feeling, Lady E?" the man asked.

Oh yes, the spiked drink. Quiti feigned dizziness. "Unsteady," she confessed. As she recalled, the drug did not render a girl unconscious, merely without much volition, so that she became amenable to whatever the man wanted, and had no memory of it the next day. An ideal one-two punch, for the man: no resistance, no recriminations.

"Oh, that's too bad. You need to lie down for a while."

"Yes," she agreed faintly. She accepted his firm hand on her elbow as he guided her to a private chamber and locked the door. Now he had her alone, drugged.

"Just relax," he said as he helped her lie down on the oh-so-convenient bed. "Let me loosen your clothes so you can breathe more easily." He got to work on her blouse, then her bra, baring her breasts. They were full and fine, with no sag.

"Oh, thank you," she said. "That's much better."

"Much better," he agreed, bending down to kiss them.

Then he worked on her skirt, carefully drawing it down and off. This presented her with a problem: she knew she could overcome him at any time, because he had no inkling of her physical strength. But she didn't want to make a nasty scene that might give someone a hint of her real identity and powers, and might also hurt Speedo's reputation, since he had brought her here. He could be accused of being in on the date rape conspiracy. She also didn't want to reveal her ability to resist.

But neither was she about to let him rape her. She had no fear of sex, but wanted it to be with a man she chose to give it to, not this impostor. Actually, a nice young man like Speedo, ironically. What was a person to make of a culture that forbade compatible sex between friends, and promoted it between enemies? But that was a question for another day. What could she do?

Now he was drawing off her panties. Whatever she was going to do, she needed to do soon, or it would be too late. Knock him out with a knee to the face? Tie him naked to the bed? Such actions would serve him right, but there would be repercussions.

The man didn't bother to remove her token mask. That was not the part of her that interested him.

Then she had on odd idea. *Hair*, she thought. *What do you recommend?*

And it answered! *Stiffen your flesh.*

She didn't quite follow that. *You do it.*

Then she felt it. Her body seemed to go into instant rigor mortis, becoming board stiff. But that still left it exposed.

Meanwhile the rake had stripped naked himself and was ready. He climbed on the bed, straddling her, his erection leading the way. Then he put his hands on her thighs, seeking to part them for more ready access. They did not part.

Surprised, he pushed harder. There was still no result. So he spread out on her, set his erect member at her secluded crotch, and shoved. And got nowhere.

Frustrated, he lifted up his body and peered closely. He took one finger and poked it at her vulva. It did not penetrate. He might as well have been addressing a plastic manikin with no apertures.

"Bitch!" he swore. He struck at her belly with his fist, as if hoping the shock would spring her legs apart and loosen her tightness. "Oww!"

For his hand might as well have struck a statue. She was unhurt, but his knuckles were evidently bruised.

The fact was, he was unable to get into her. He surely had never anticipated being balked in quite this manner.

She couldn't resist taunting him. "What's the matter, honey? Lost your interest?"

In a fury he jumped on her, trying to choke her around the neck. She barely felt the pressure.

"If you're not going to do it, I'm going to go back and dance."

He sought to strike her face, but she blocked him with her wrist and shoved him aside. She sat up. "You're having a bad dream, honey. Maybe you'd better sleep it off."

He tried once more to grab her. This time she put her fingers on special touch points on his neck and pressed in. He dropped, unconscious.

There was one more talent she hadn't known she had: the knowledge of key pressure points, and the ability to use them. She must have read about it, and forgotten, but now was resurrecting the information.

Quiti quickly dressed, checking herself in the wall mirror. Then she picked up the rake's clothing, tucked it under her arm, and departed. He would have a problem attending the dance without it. She returned to her table just as Speedo did. "Let's dance," she said, setting down the clothing.

"You okay?" he asked, concerned.

"I just needed to freshen up. I'm fine." Why tell him? There was no need for him to know.

They finished the evening in good order. "That was one great date!" Speedo said as they exited the hall. "Thank you!"

"You're welcome. I learned things." Such as several new properties of her growing hair. What would it be capable of when it grew to full length? In fact, what *was* its full length? She had no idea.

"Maybe we can do it again some time," he said hopefully.

"Maybe," she agreed. "Certainly we can do more meals together."

They walked on toward their homes, hand in hand. It was a wonderful evening.

# CHAPTER 4:
## *Arsenal*

Two days later they met again for the big noon meal. Joe saw them coming. "Do you care much what you eat, so long as there's a lot of it? There's stuff I'll give you free, if you want it."

Quiti looked around, and saw he had fresh potato salad and mashed potato. "Like new potato peels before they go in the garbage?"

"Well, they're sanitary. I noticed you ate the cores of apples and chewed up plumb pits, leaving nothing behind. You have a hunger like none I've seen before."

"We'll take them."

"It's not my business, but—"

Quiti read his mood. He was well meaning but curious. "Come join us in the booth, when you have time, and we'll tell you about it. But you have to commit to secrecy."

"Fair enough."

He did join them when there was a lull. "Tell him," Quiti told Speedo.

"But he might believe it."

"We can trust him."

So while Quiti gulped down a mass of potato peelings, Speedo told Joe about her visit to the warehouse and encounter with the hairball. "So now she's growing this real special hair, real fast, and it's giving her strength and brains and beauty, and we think it's even curing her cancer, but it makes her hungry as hell," he concluded.

"That's some story," Joe agreed. "I'm not sure I believe it, though."

Quiti glanced at him and flashed her hair blue.

"And I'm not sure I don't," Joe said, amazed.

"Want to arm wrestle me to test my strength?"

"Don't do it," Speedo said quickly. "She's like a gorilla. I mean, not in her looks; her power."

Joe shook his head. "I know you, Quiti. I know all the kids who come here. You were shy and quiet. I know that you are, or maybe were, terminal. You always were a bit chubby, and no beauty. I see the changes in you. You're not shy anymore! If the hair is doing it, it's changing you every which way. But alien hairball or no, I don't see how you can eat so much and not get fat."

"I'm not getting fat." She glanced around, making sure there were no other diners in sight, then opened her blouse, which she had kept both loose and tight: loose around the bust and belly, tight around her neck, so as to hide her body. She showed him her supremely fit torso and well mounted breasts. "Same story with the butt and legs. It's all going to the hair. It's hardly over an inch long, but it must weigh half a pound, and it's growing."

"I am impressed," Joe said. "You have been transformed." Then he frowned. "Why are you confiding in me? You certainly didn't have to."

Quiti nodded as she finished the last of the peels and wiped her mouth clean. "Same reason I confided in Speedo. I don't know exactly where I'm headed, but it's obvious I can't do it alone. I need safe bases, people I can trust, who won't judge me or try to rape me."

"Rape!" Speedo exclaimed. "I'd never—"

"At ease," Joe said. "I think I know what she's referring

to. We pick up a lot of gossip here, as people relax and talk."

"But—"

Quiti smiled. "Tell him," she said to Joe.

"You went to the dance with a special anonymous date, a beauty," Joe said. "I didn't know who she was until she showed me her body just now. There was a set-up. They lured you out of the way, and a punk drugged her drink with a roofie and took her into a back room. We don't know what happened, but pretty soon she emerged and resumed dancing with you, as if nothing had happened, but that bad man wasn't found until next morning, naked and alone. He wouldn't say what occurred; he was just glad to get his clothing back." He glanced at Quiti. "What did happen?"

"I didn't want to make a scene. I could have fought him off; in fact I could have pulverized him. The drink didn't incapacitate me. So I simply put him to sleep and took his clothes, figuring he wouldn't be candid about the details."

"I didn't know!" Speedo said.

"I didn't want to mess up your evening."

"But he tried to rape you!"

"Tried, yes. He didn't succeed."

"This is pretty personal stuff," Joe said. "Thank you for trusting me. But don't gamble like that with others; not everyone can be trusted."

"It was no gamble."

"Quiti, you can't judge a man by his face. There are some who will lie to you with perfect conviction."

"One more secret: I can read minds, or at least moods. That's how I knew that rapist was bad news from the start, and that you're okay."

"Reading minds? You mean telepathy?"

"Or something like it. It's the hair, again; it's doing things to my brain. Good things."

New customers entered the eatery. "Gotta go," Joe said, rising. "But thanks. I'll keep your secret." He moved off.

"How did you stop him?" Speedo demanded. "That rapist?"

"We were naked. I made my skin tough, and he couldn't get in."

"Tough?"

"I was like a plastic doll. Nothing budged."

He sighed. "At least he got to try."

"Speedo, I told you why I can't let you—"

"I guess you know I got a crush on you. You can read my mind."

"I know," she agreed. "If I was going to have sex with anyone, I'd like it to be you, not a loser like him. But I can't do it."

"Statutory," he said sadly.

He was really hurting. She couldn't blame him; he lacked the perspective that came with maturity. Most of what he had was hormones. She wished she could accommodate him. But she was not about to break the law. She made a decision. "But I think I owe you. I will let you try, even though it's bound to just frustrate you worse."

He seemed to have difficulty crediting this. "You'll let me try?"

"We'll get naked together, and I won't resist at all, except for the hardening. Then you'll see how it is."

"Okay!"

They left the eatery. They walked to his house, which was empty during the day. They entered and went to his bedroom. They both stripped naked. He had a rigid erection.

She lay on the bed, supine, and spread her legs. "Try," she said.

"Remember, you said I could!"

"Could try," she agreed.

He got on her eagerly and tried. She firmed her flesh where it counted. He pushed, but got bent aside. There simply was no access. It was as though she were a doll with the externals in place but no internals. Ridges without apertures. He was wasting his time. "Damn!"

"You may kiss me," she said. "Stroke me."

"Where?"

"Anywhere."

He kissed her mouth, and she kissed him back. Then he kissed her breasts, and they remained supple. Her rounded belly, filled with what she had just eaten. Her leather-firm groin. "Damn!"

He was crying. She put her arms around him, drew him up against her, and held him close, comforting him. "I'm so sorry, Speedo. I know how badly you want it. I shouldn't be teasing you."

"Damn," he said into her breasts.

And yet she read in his mind that his frustration was not complete. He loved her, and was more than willing to be with her this way than not at all. She was giving him half a loaf. It was a necessary compromise.

In due course he roused himself, and they both dressed. "You did warn me. I know you're just doing what's right. But—"

"Yes, we can do it again some time," she agreed. The crisis was over, at least for the time being.

"Quiti, I just want to be with you, any way I can. Can I help you any other way?"

"Actually, yes. I've been thinking that I could unexpectedly find myself caught somewhere, maybe being chased, and need to escape. I'm getting new power from my hair; I think it reaches into my brain, and my brain sends hormones or whatever into my body, making it toughen up. But this mood reading—if it's the preliminary to real telepathy, I want to use it. May I try to read your mind?"

"Sure. But all you'll find there is an image of you, looking like a goddess. That's not even my imagination, it's memory."

"I'm thinking of reading specific thoughts. Could you think of things, and I'll try to read them? I mean, things other than sex."

"Aww." But he cooperated. "I've got a mental picture."

She focused. There was something, but it was a blur. She brought her head close to his, and it clarified. "It's a—a vacuum cleaner!"

"Got it!" He was as delighted as she. "Here's another."

She stepped back, orienting on the blur. This time it clarified a little farther away than the first had. "A church bell."

"Right! Here's another."

The blur formed into a picture of two heads, kissing. "All right, this once," she agreed, and kissed him.

"You got telepathy," he said. "I wish I had it."

"I wonder. There may be an equivalent. Let me try thought projection."

"My mind's open."

She formed a mental picture of a coiled rattlesnake, and tried to send it to him.

"I'm getting something, but I don't know what," he said. "Maybe a hangman's noose?"

"It was a rattlesnake. At least you got the coiling."

"Maybe when your hair gets longer, you'll have more power."

"Maybe," she agreed, wondering. As yet she had no idea of the limits, but the hair effects were getting stronger day by day.

"Your hair—it can change color," he said. "Joe almost flipped when you turned it blue. But can it do more?"

"More?"

"Like maybe invisible?"

She made the hair fade out, so that her scalp seemed bald. "I do that all the time, to conceal its presence and rapid growth."

"I know. 'Cause it doesn't like the wig, when there's sunlight." He paused. "Sunlight! It must have more power then."

"It must," she agreed.

They went outside. "But I was thinking, could it make not just itself, but you invisible? So you could escape when you needed to."

"That's a stretch," she said dubiously.

"Try it again. Invisible."

She concentrated. "You'll have to tell me whether—" She paused, for he was staring. "What is it?"

"You got a mirror?"

She dug into her purse and found her compact. She fished out the little mirror and offered it to him.

"No, you use it. Look at yourself."

She humored him. She held the mirror before her face and looked into it.

And almost dropped it.

There was nothing there. Her body was there, but above her shoulders there was emptiness. Her head was invisible.

"You're the headless woman," he said, awed. "It even takes out your face."

"The effect must extend a little beyond the hair itself," she said, similarly awed.

"I can see the house behind you. It's as if your head isn't there. It's not blocking out the light or anything, it's just gone."

"Let's make sure. Kiss me."

"Sure! Anytime." He stepped close and kissed her face. He missed her mouth slightly and got part of her cheek and nose. Then he corrected by feel and centered on her mouth. She could feel his joy of the occasion.

"So my head is still here," she said as he broke.

"It sure is. But I still can't see it." She canceled the effect. "Now I see it," he said.

"So you were right about the sunlight. It makes the effect stronger."

"Stronger," he agreed. "First time I ever kissed an invisible woman."

"I think that's enough for now," she said. "I need to go home and assimilate what I have learned in the last hour. Thank you."

"Anytime!"

After that they practiced a bit more each day. Quiti got so she could make Speedo see the coiled rattlesnake. Then she managed to put the snake on the ground. She worked on other images, like a giant scorpion, a splash of vomit, a fallen anvil, a ball of slime, an alligator, and an armed grenade. Any of those should make a pursuer pause in his tracks.

"How about a nude?" Speedo suggested.

"You have a one track mind."

"No, I mean it. Chances are it'll be a man chasing you. If there's one thing to make him stop and look, it's a naked woman. A snake he might try to bash, but a woman he'd stop to look at."

"A nude," she said thoughtfully. "You may have a point."

"Make her look like Lady Excelsior."

"That's a self portrait!"

"Sure. Should be easy for you to do. And not a giveaway, because you keep your body covered now so folk won't see the changes in it."

"I'll try it." Later she crafted the nude, in her bedroom, standing naked before the tall mirror. She turned slightly, trying to get new angles, and finally set up a mirror behind so that she could view her rear aspect too. She wanted a holographic image, distracting from any direction. Once she had it, she concentrated on making it look alive, instead of being a still statue. On breathing. Quivering as it walked. Glancing around. Hair flouncing enticingly.

She showed Speedo. "Oh, god, Quiti, I wish I could take that to bed! I bet it's not plastic hard where it counts."

"It's not solid at all," she reminded him. "You can't touch it physically."

"Oh. Yeah. I guess there's no substitute for the real thing."

"But as a distraction, it should be fine," she said. "Thank you for the idea."

The day of her routine MRI appointment came. She had to go into the hospital to have them photograph the inside of her head, checking the progress of the dread brain cancer. Was it still there? She very much wanted to know.

They set her up in the machine. But there was a problem. "It's fuzzy," the technician said. "Are you wearing a metal mesh or something?"

"You can see that I'm not," Quiti said.

"A skull cap? Something is interfering with the field."

Suddenly Quiti knew it was the hair, which was now two inches long. It could change its appearance from the outside. That meant it could interfere with the light bouncing off it. It must be messing up the magnetic field too. Why hadn't she anticipated that? It was obvious in retrospect. "Maybe your machine has a glitch."

"Maybe," the tech agreed dubiously. "It was working fine on the person just before you."

Quiti got out of the chair. "I'll come back another time."

"Wait! We'll get it straight."

But she was already on her way out. Coming here had been a mistake. What had she been thinking -? If her cancer was gone, they would be all over her to figure out why. If it wasn't, she was doomed anyway. She had nothing to gain here, and plenty to lose, like her freedom. Because if she really had suffered a miracle cure, after being firmly diagnosed terminal, they would never let her go. She'd be effectively a prisoner in a laboratory, subject to endless study. She didn't want that. In fact she couldn't afford it; she knew she had an important future, one set up by the hairball, and she wanted to reach it.

An alarm sounded, reminiscent of a prisoner escaping. They were closing in already. She hurried toward the exit.

A man appeared in the hallway ahead. "Stop, miss! You haven't been cleared to leave!"

What to do? She stared him in the face, orienting on his mind. Then she projected the Nude illusion.

The orderly stopped, staring at the image. Quiti could see only its outline; it was his brain that was generating it, while her mind served mainly to place it. But she knew exactly what he was seeing.

She sidled past him and resumed progress toward the door. But then a nurse appeared. "You can't—" she started.

Quiti met her eye and projected the rattlesnake. The woman screamed.

Then Quiti was past her and out. She ran to her parent's car and got in, grabbing her cell phone. "Mom, I'm through," she said urgently. "I'm in the car."

"Already?"

"Yes. Let's go home now."

Her mother emerged from the waiting room. She walked slowly toward the car. *Hurry!*

The door opened behind her. "Wait!" a man called.

Could she do it at this range? Quiti leaned forward in the car, focusing on the man's head. She projected the alligator.

The man paused. Was he seeing it?

He stepped back, his mouth forming on O of surprise. Yes!

Betty had paused when the man called, but now resumed progress, as she was not seeing any alligator. She got into the car. "Why didn't you meet me in the waiting room, dear?" she asked.

"I was in such a hurry to get home, I forgot." Close enough to the truth.

"Did they tell you the result?"

"They never have results at the time," Quiti reminded her. "They have to develop and analyze the pictures first. But this time there was a glitch, so they couldn't do it."

"Then we should make another appointment."

"We can do that by phone. Let's just go now."

"Of course, dear."

They made it safely home, to Quiti's immense relief. Betty made a new appointment by phone. The next day's newspaper had no mention of a disturbance, and certainly not of a nude woman in the hall, a rattlesnake, or alligator. Evidently the folk who had experienced these things thought they were exactly what they were: illusions, and did not want to embarrass themselves by publicizing them.

Speedo found the whole thing hilarious. "You used the spooks! They worked! I wish I had seen their faces!"

"My arsenal really paid off," Quiti agreed, similarly pleased.

"But now they know something's up."

"I can't afford to go back to the lab," she agreed. "But what can I do?"

"Damn," he said. "You'll have to disappear, at least until your hair finishes growing. Then maybe you'll be so sharp with the special effects that you can return as Lady Excelsior or someone else and they won't know it's you."

"You're right. I'll go tonight."

"I figured that. That's what I hate."

"Hide me tonight, maybe in your room. Don't tell your folks. I will sleep with you." She held up a warning finger. "As Excelsior, with the plastic flesh. You can have at me all night as I sleep, if you want to, with that one limit."

"I'll take it," he said sadly. "But maybe, if I'm of age when you return—"

She laughed. "I'll turn off the plastic flesh. I owe it to you, for the help you have given me."

"I love helping you!"

"And I have taken advantage of that, in my desperation. It is time to return your life to you."

"Time," he agreed. "I know it, but it hurts."

She told her parents. "I may have had a miraculous remission of my cancer. They will want to lock me in the hospital and study me forever. I couldn't stand that. So I will have to leave you tonight, and disappear. I promise I'll send you messages so you'll know I'm all right. But I must go."

"Quiti!" her mother wailed.

"She's right, Betty," Bill said. "We can see how healthy she's become. She's not going to die. But they'll never let her go. She has to hide, at least for now." He looked at Quiti. "We don't have much extra money."

"I'll get by," Quiti said quickly. "I'll find ways."

"You can't use your credit card or your cell phone; those will track you. And how will you message us, without giving away your location?"

Quiti thought fast. "You know the neighbor boy, Speedo? I'll send him messages to relay to you. And Joe, of Joe's Eatery. You can trust what they tell you, and it won't be traceable."

"But we'd so much rather have you with us," Betty said tearfully.

"Mom, you faced the loss of me, completely. Now I'm going to live, but apart from you. Isn't that better?"

"Yes." But she looked none too certain.

Quiti packed efficiently, taking only one solid bag. She left her cell phone and credit card behind. She had a good dinner. Then as darkness came, she kissed them both and departed.

She circled the block, her mind ranging out to be sure no one was noticing her, and came to Speedo's house. *I'm here*, she thought to him.

He came out immediately, and ushered her inside and to his bedroom. She stripped and got into his bed without comment. He stripped and joined her. "I know it's no go," he whispered. "But I can't help trying."

"I hate teasing you like this, but it's all I can offer you." Then while he kissed her mouth and breasts, she told him the rest. "I know your mind better than any other, because of the interaction we have had. I believe I can communicate with you telepathically from a distance. I will send you messages for my folks that you can relay, so I can't be traced. Will you do that?"

"Yes! Anything."

"The messages should get stronger with practice, and as my hair grows."

"I'll live for them."

"Speedo, get a girlfriend. You know I was never destined to be that for you. But our connection is in certain ways more intimate. It's friendship with unusual benefits."

"I know it, even though I wish it were more."

She did not argue that case. "Now I must get my sleep. You have the freedom of my body, with the limit."

"Yes."

She slept. She could do that now, as if clicking a switch.

In the morning, before dawn, she woke refreshed. Speedo woke the moment she stirred. "Quiti—"

"You know I must go." She got up, used the bathroom, and dressed.

"It's not that. You need to know this. I kissed your hair—and it kissed me back."

She looked at him. "Say again?"

"Read my mind to verify it. It's sort of love you, love your hair; that's what makes you what you are. So I kissed it beside your ear, and I swear it formed lips and kissed me back, passionately. And it sent me a thought: *there will be a*

36

*role for you."*

It was true; his mind did verify it. "My hair likes you," she said in wonder.

"Yes. And it gave me the patience and courage to let you go, except for your messages. I can do that now."

"I'm glad." Indeed, it was a huge relief. She had paid for his help in the only way she could, but had hated teasing him.

She departed as dawn was just arriving, keeping to the shadows. Her new life was upon her, whatever it might be. She knew it would work out, because her hair thought so. She owed everything to the hair.

# CHAPTER 5:
## *Gena*

"What now, hair?" she asked rhetorically as she walked to the nearest through street. And the hair answered, in its fashion, sending her thoughts ranging out through the neighborhood, seeking certain minds. She waited, letting it do its thing. The experience Speedo had had, getting kissed by the hair, had to be significant: the hair had shown self will, independent of her awareness, though it had surely drawn on her dozing brain. It was another confirmation that the alien hairball had given her not a toy flute, but an orchestra. She had left her wig behind, as she no longer needed it; the hair could make her seem to have a head of short dark locks, or little blond curls. At the moment she had a red cap with brown wisps peeking out from beneath. The rest of her outfit was modest, masking her attributes to the extent feasible without denying her femininity: heavy outdoor plaid shirt, canvas skirt, sneakers.

*There.* Before she knew it she was stepping out onto the edge of the street, flagging down an approaching motorist. The car screeched to a halt, and she opened the passenger door and climbed in.

"Where you going, miss?" the driver asked. "I almost didn't see you." He was a middle aged man. His mind was benign; he was not about to try to molest any woman.

"Isn't there a truck stop cafeteria a few miles along? I heard they were hiring waitresses. That's what I'm looking for."

"There sure is. I'm going right past it. Good thing you caught me. It's almost like fate."

"Almost," she agreed. There was no coincidence to it; the hair evidently had known where he was going as well as that he was no threat to her.

They chatted amicably. He seemed glad of the passing company, especially of a pretty girl.

"There it is, miss," he said, and pulled to a stop outside the cafeteria. There were several big rigs in its capacious parking lot. This was definitely the place. "Good luck with the job."

"Thank you so much." She leaned across and kissed his ear. "It would have been a long walk."

Thrilled by the kiss, he drove on. Quiti reflected momentarily on the way her life had changed. Pre-hairball, her innocent kiss would have thrilled no one.

She walked to the entrance and stepped inside. Four tables were occupied by men, one by a woman. She went to the woman, assessing her on the way: about 30, long dark hair, brown eyes, and shapely. She was, it seemed, a long-haul driver.

Quiti paused at the table. "I have committed no crime. I'm not a criminal or a prostitute. I have a serious need to avoid discovery in a setting I can trust. I have money for my own needs, and I don't care where I go. I can be dropped off anywhere you choose, at any time, and I promise to make no fuss. Could you use a traveling companion?"

The woman eyed her cannily. "You les?"

"No, hetero. But saving it for the right man."

"You've got a shape on you. This is a rough neighborhood, long-hauling cross country. Ninety five percent male."

"I can defend myself if necessary."

"Can you drive?"

"Yes. I've never touched a rig, but I'm a very fast learner when I need to be."

"You were looking for me."

"I'm looking for someone who meets my need. I believe you are the one."

The woman laughed. "I've never heard that pickup line used by a woman before. Not on another woman. Go your way; you'll be better off riding with a man."

"Let me show you a trick," Quiti said, looking her in the eye. Then, having zeroed in on the woman's mind, she projected a sample illusion. It was a small fire blazing in the middle of the table. "It's not real," Quiti said. "No one else can see it. Pass your hand through it."

Cautiously, the woman did. "No heat!"

"A token hallucination. I am not an ordinary person."

The woman was clearly impressed. "I've never met a stage magician before."

"No stage props. No sleight of hand. It's mental. Not something I care to advertise."

"Okay, you got my attention. Will you tell me your story? I can keep my mouth shut."

"As we drive."

Now she smiled. "Of course. Okay, it's a deal. Ride with me 'till you bore me. Sit down."

"Thank you." Quiti drew out the opposite chair and seated herself.

The waitress approached. "Your morning special," Quiti said. "Doubled."

"Pay for it first." Evidently not every trucker could be trusted.

Quiti paid for it, then settled down to talk with the woman while the order was in process. "Shall we exchange introductions? I am Quiti, age twenty, single, three weeks into the most remarkable adventure I never heard of."

"Gena. Thirty. Single, sort of. Driver. It's mostly dull work."

"Hello, Gena. I am very glad to meet you."

"How do you know I won't slip you a mickey, rob you, and dump you on the highway in your briefs?"

"I can read your mind, or at least your mood and nature. I know I can trust you. You're a good person."

"You're guessing."

"No."

"How smart are you, Quiti?"

"I'm probably the smartest person you'll ever encounter. But that's coincidental. I was a grade C student in school, and remain at heart a dull ordinary person. I was never a geek until recently."

"How honest are you?"

"I try to be ethically perfect, but it's difficult in an imperfect world. I won't lie to you, steal from you, or seek to do you harm. But I am hiding from the authorities, and will have to lie to conceal my true identity."

"You will tell me why."

"I will tell you everything you want to know, trusting your discretion, when we are private."

"What do you think of me, based on what little you know of me?"

"I think you are a nice person who has struggled with a moral issue without a perfect resolution. Who does her best regardless. The kind of person I'd like to have for a friend."

"And you can read my mind."

"Your mood. I can't get specific thoughts unless they are directed at me. But in time, with a friend, yes, I could read your mind."

"I'm choosy about my friends."

"Yes. I hope I can qualify."

Quiti's order arrived, a double dose of pancakes,

scrambled eggs, milk, and sweet rolls. She piled into it, soon eating every part of it.

"You eat like two stevedores," Gena remarked as she sipped her coffee.

"That, too, I will explain when we are private."

In due course they moved out to the rig. "I'm hauling machine parts to a factory in Connecticut," Gena said. "Several days' drive. Dull as hell."

"That's fine with me. I have no destination other than anonymity."

Gena cranked up the rig, and pulled slowly out of the lot. Quiti sat beside her, looking around.

Once they were out on the highway and traveling at speed, Gena spoke again. "I've got a notion that your story is more complicated than mine, so I'll tell mine first."

"Fair enough." The morning sun was out now, and Quiti angled her head so that her hair got the brunt of it.

"I was a history student your age when I discovered I was pregnant. I didn't believe in abortions; I mean, a baby in the belly is not just a lump of protoplasm, it's a person, still forming, and deserves its chance at life. I was not about to marry, and not just because my weasel of a boyfriend disappeared about ten seconds after he learned I was gravid. He was wrong for me, and would never make a good father. So I decided to put it up for adoption, but not anonymously. I wanted an open adoption, so I could participate in the life of my child, even if I couldn't keep it myself. It used to be that the sadistic adoption agencies put up rafts of walls to prevent the donor mother from ever knowing anything about her baby. They sure wanted to punish her for the sin of careless sex. But we're getting beyond that anal retention attitude now, and more than half of adoptions today are open. Am I boring you yet?"

"No! This is new to me."

"I researched, and did due diligence, and chose the

adoptive family myself from a number of prospects. We made a formal agreement that I could maintain lifelong contact with my daughter, as she turned out to be. They named her Idola, meaning a lovely vision. It was perfect. I did my part; I nursed my baby for the first six months, though she lived with her new family, not with me. We all wanted her to have as healthy a start in her life as possible, and that meant staying off the bottle, and no one else could nurse her. It was wonderful! I truly loved her." She sighed. "And therein lay mischief. When I nursed her, I bonded with her. I didn't want to give her up. She was with a good family, and they were doing everything right, and I knew I had no business even thinking of reneging on the agreement. It would be a serious breach of trust on my part. I couldn't take care of her on my own anyway; I'd just mess up her life. So I hung on as the years passed, being Auntie Gena, though the child knew the real story. But that sense of loss never faded. So what was I to do with my irrational impractical longing? I didn't trust myself. I knew I had to wean myself away from her, to be rid of the guilty temptation."

"I never dreamed of such a situation," Quiti said. "But of course I never expected to have a child of my own anyway."

"That's why I took this job as a long hauler. It takes me across the country, far away for weeks and sometimes months. But in my case absence really does make the heart grow fonder. All I think about is Idola. She's nine now, a lovely girl. I long to see her again, but also dread it, because I know it will stir up the guilty longing."

"So all you need is to be able to interact with her normally, but without the wicked temptation," Quiti said.

"That's it. If it hasn't faded in nine years, when is it ever going to?"

Quiti remembered how her hair had eased Speedo's longing, so that he could live with the situation. "There might be a way. But I'd have to study it further."

"Your turn. What's so special about you, and I'm not being sarcastic."

Quiti told her the story, beginning with the alien hairball. "So I think I've lost the cancer," she concluded. "But I can't get it tested. I'll just have to see if my health holds."

"You're right. That's weird," Gena said. "And that fabulous hair of yours just might be able to ease my wrongheaded longing."

"It might," Quiti agreed. "But I could have interpreted it all wrong, just wanted to make it easier on Speedo."

"We can test it now."

"Now? But your daughter is far away."

"Yes. But the problem is not with her. She's fine with the way things are. It's with me. I'm the one who needs to change. Maybe I can touch your hair and find out."

"I suppose that's possible," Quiti agreed, surprised. "For the genius I seem to be, I can still miss the obvious."

"Geniuses are notorious for that."

"Well, we can try it, but I'm afraid you'll be disappointed."

"I'll be disappointed if I don't at least try."

"Yes." At least they could do that much.

Gena pulled the truck into a secluded lane and parked it. "May I touch your hair?"

As if they were making out, there in the cab of the rig! "Go ahead."

Gena reached out tentatively and touched it. "Oh, my!" She drew back her hand.

"What?"

"It tingled."

"I didn't feel that."

"Maybe you're too much a part of it. May I try again?"

"Certainly. Maybe—now don't get me wrong; I'm thinking of Speedo—you should kiss it. Get your head really close so it is in range. And focus on what you want to accomplish. I really don't know to what extent the hair has its own volition. I think it mainly interacts with my brain and body."

Gena leaned toward her, hesitated, then put her mouth to the side of Quiti's head. She kissed the hair. "Oh!"

"What happened?"

"It kissed me back! And—"

"Yes?"

"I can live without Idola. I love her, I want to stay in her life, but I don't want to take her away from it. I don't want to interfere with her happiness. I want just to be Auntie Gena, as I was supposed to be."

This was hard to believe. "Are you serious? You're not just saying it?"

"Read my mind," Gena said seriously.

Quiti did. There was peace there. The tension was gone. "It seems to be true."

"You bet it's true! Oh, Quiti, I love your hair!"

Quiti was trying to sort this out emotionally. "That's good. Because it's going to grow, and gain power, and I'd like to be with you while it does."

"Oh, yes! I want to help it and you all I can. To see it achieve its full glory."

"Are you sure it didn't tune you into what it wants? Rather than what you want? There could be a downside."

"If it did, I'm amenable. My life has been dull. I already know that it will never be dull with you."

Quiti spread her hands. "I hope it is for the best."

"Oh, it is. I know it."

They resumed motion. Gena was evidently quite satisfied, but Quiti remained uncertain. If the hair could change people's underlying drives, what else might it do? Was it really helping her, enhancing her life, or was she a mere pawn in some larger game?

The hairball had seemed benign. Was it really? She wished she could be sure.

"So are we on for the duration?" Quiti asked. "I mean, for the next year?"

"Oh, yes. I want you in my life."

"I am satisfied with that. But I am frankly uneasy about the way my hair seems to have affected your mind. It's almost like a romantic relationship based on superficial attraction. It may not last."

"It's not romantic. It will last. It's clear that you have not experienced the power of your hair."

"Oh, I have. It turned me from suicide to boldly positive. But I'm wearing it, so its continuing power is not surprising."

"Hair power. I never dreamed I'd encounter anything like it, but I do like it."

Quiti shrugged. "If you are satisfied, so am I. If you change your mind, just let me know."

"I won't change my mind. But Quiti, if you should change yours, or circumstances require you to move on, can I move with you? Continue as your friend?"

"If you want to." Then she thought of something. "I'll need money. I said I'd pay my own way, and I will, but I was thinking shorter term. I'll need to find a way to get moderate amounts without violating any laws or cheating anyone. I don't want to sell my body, either."

"You could get a damn good price for your body."

"No."

Gena nodded, understanding. "Can your hair help there? Put on illusions for pay?"

"I don't want to attract attention to my hair. The whole point in being with you is to be able to develop whatever powers the hair has as it grows, without any authority or greedy person knowing."

"There is something. It's not exactly illegal, but strictly

off the record. Sometimes a trucker will give someone a long distance lift, Uber-style. There are places where they make connections. I know of one in the next town."

"A man could be trouble. He'd see two attractive women."

"Don't I know it! But how about a woman? She might not want to ride with a male trucker, even if he offered to do it for free. Same reason you and I don't."

Quiti nodded. "That might work. But that would be your contribution rather than mine. I'm trying to be financially independent, no burden to you."

"Maybe, maybe not. We could try it and see. You can have the money, regardless."

"Let's try it once. If I don't do my share, I won't do it again."

In due course Gena pulled into the lot of an unimpressive diner. "We're hungry anyway," she said. "It's lunch time. I've stopped here before. The food's not great, but there's plenty and it's cheap."

"That's the kind I need."

They went to the counter and ordered. Then Gena broached the matter. "Anyone need a lift east? We're not looking for a man."

The proprietor studied them a moment. "There is one waiting. A child. She has to go from her father to her mother, 400 miles away. But she can be difficult. So can her dad. You'd have to meet them."

"Bring them here," Gena said. "Meanwhile we'll eat."

While they were waiting for the food, two men came in. They spied the two women immediately and nodded as they gave their order.

"Crap," Gena swore. "They'll be hitting on us. We'll have to back them off."

"I have an idea. Take your spoon and make like you're scooping something off the table and eating it."

"You're up to something."

"Indeed. An illusion. I hope it works.

When the men completed their order they headed right for the women. Quiti caught the eye of one, then the other, and sent one of her prepared projections. Then she joined Gena, eating air from the table.

The men came close and paused, staring. Then they moved on to the farthest other table without saying a word. The crisis was over.

"What are we eating?" Gena asked.

"Spilled vomit."

Gena dropped her spoon, looking momentarily sick. Then she laughed. "No wonder they changed their minds! They didn't want to kiss our mouths."

"I thought that might be the case."

The proprietor brought their meal. "I made the call. They'll be here soon."

"Thank you," Gena said.

Quiti rapidly packed away three quarters of it, Gena cooperating, and they were done by the time the ride seekers arrived, a man and a rather pretty girl child. The proprietor gestured to their table. "This is the pickup we want," Quiti murmured.

"Sit down," Gena told them. "I'm Gena, a long haul trucker, and this is my companion Quiti. We're following the highway due east for a thousand miles. You need a ride?"

"Maybe," the man said. "This is Fifi. She's five. She doesn't much like strangers." And the girl was staring rebelliously at them.

Quiti caught her eye. "Touch my hair," she said.

Surprised, Fifi did. Her eyes widened. Then she got up and hugged Quiti, crying tears of relief.

"We like children," Gena explained. "Children like us."

Amazed, the man did not even ask for references. He gave Gena a card with the delivery address, and money to cover the trip. "Her bag is in the car. She has a sandwich and pop. I will call her mother." He departed, leaving the child with them.

Soon they were on their way, Fifi sitting on the wide seat between the two of them. Now she was talkative, interested in the truck and the passing scenery. The single touch of Quiti's hair had transformed her. Satisfied, Quiti positioned herself to intercept as much sunlight as possible. She felt better when she did that, knowing it was the hair sharing its satisfaction.

Gena answered the child's myriad questions, and Quiti realized that though the woman was now prepared to live with the situation with her daughter, she remained hungry for a daughter's company. This child was that, for the moment.

"You like the sun," Fifi said to Quiti.

"I do. It's good for my hair."

"Stay in the sun," the child advised.

In three hours they stopped for a snack and restroom facilities, especially for the child. Gena saw to her in the lady's room, not leaving her alone in any strange place. She was obviously experienced with daughters. She bought her an ice cream cone. Quiti didn't comment.

Then Gena broached something. "Do you care to drive, Quiti? It's okay in this state as long as you're competent, and I'm with you."

Surprised, Quiti agreed. "I can, once you familiarize me with the controls and the rules of the road. If you really want to trust your expensive rig to me."

"I'm ready. It's insured."

So Quiti drove, quickly mastering the nuances. She glanced at her companions, and discovered Fifi sitting on Gena's lap, resting against her bosom. Soon she was asleep—and so was Gena.

That was why Quiti was driving. To let Gena have her

heart's desire for the occasion.

It was nine in the evening when they drew to a halt by Fifi's mother's house. Her mother was standing outside, waiting for them. Fifi ran to hug her, bursting with news about the wonderful big truck trip. "I've never seen her like this," the woman confided. "I feared the trip would be traumatic for her."

"She was no trouble at all," Gena said.

"She liked my hair," Quiti said.

"Hair!" Fifi exclaimed happily. "Sun!"

The three adults exchanged a glance, bemused, albeit for different reasons.

"You girls must have something to eat," the mother said. "I'm so pleased you made the trip easy for Fifi."

So they had a late supper with her and the child, and it was good. When it was done, and time to move on, Fifi hugged and kissed each of them. "I hope it's you again, when I have to go back to Daddy," she said.

Gena considered. "It might be. We go back and forth, depending on the loads."

"I'll give you the schedule," the mother said. "It will be spring, after school closes. She spends the summers with him. She loves it, except for the traveling with strangers."

"They're not strangers," Fifi said.

"We'll try," Gena promised. Quiti knew she was serious.

Back on the road, Gena driving, Quiti with the money, they discussed it again. "You were satisfied with the deal," Quiti said. It wasn't a question.

"You know it. To hold a child again—that's heaven."

"Next time it may not be a child."

"A woman would do, not that I would hug her. Or even a man, if your hair tamed him."

"How do you feel about being with a man, just in passing?"

"I'm amenable, if I like him. Just so long as the decision

is mine, not his. You?"

"I'm satisfied to wait, at least until my hair fills out. As far as I'm concerned, this is all about the hair."

"Fair enough. If we transport a man, and he's interesting, I'll take him on. But you, with your youth and figure—you may have to turn him off you and onto me."

"I think I can do that, or rather the hair can. With luck he'll never know he's been swapped."

They laughed together. They understood each other.

Then Quiti remembered her promise to send news to her parents. As she rode, she focused on Speedo. She hadn't originally figured on going this far away from home. Could she reach him? Yes! He had accepted her departure, but his love for her remained. It made him an eager receptor for her mental beacon. *Hairpower here,* she thought. *I am far away but in good hands. I will send again another day.* That was it, but she trusted it was enough.

Gena drove to midnight, then parked in a rest area. "No sense pushing it to the danger point," Gena said. "Unless I'm in a hurry because of a deadline, I prefer to drive safely. There's a bed behind the seat; do you want it?"

"It's your rig. Should we take turns guarding it?"

"I sleep light. I also think that your hair can be alert."

"Yes. It will wake me if there is any near approach."

"I love your hair."

They took turns using the facility, then Gena slept on the little bed and Quiti stretched out on the seat.

It had been a remarkable day, but a good one. A very good one.

# CHAPTER 6:
## *Hair Skirt*

They delivered the tools to the machine shop, then picked up a cargo of mattresses destined for Florida. Each day Quiti sent a message to Speedo, reassuring him and her folks that she was well and happy. She did not say exactly where she was, lest someone or some computer catch on and check the location of Gena's rig, but she did let him know she was on the Eastern coast.

Three weeks had passed on the road, and Quiti's hair was now four inches long. Gena had developed almost as much of a passion for exploring the new hair power parameters as Quiti herself had.

There was no immediate load or destination available in Florida, but they were glad for the time off. They parked not far from a beach, and went swimming in their underwear. There were other vacationers on the beach, but any who looked curious lost their interest after meeting Quiti's gaze.

The hair absolutely loved the Florida sun. Quiti was concerned about getting burned on her bare shoulders, but discovered that the hair was fluffing out, intercepting the sunlight before much of it struck her skin. Was this to protect her from sunburn, or to deliver more energy to the hair? Did it matter?

What would the hair think of the salt water? Quiti had

discovered early on that the hair did not like to be washed. It repelled water and soap, so that none touched her scalp. When she had gotten caught briefly in a summer shower, the hair had not gotten wet. Now she damn well proposed to swim. Would the hair freak out?

"Last one in's a rotten tomato!" Gena cried as she splashed into the shallow water. Quiti saw how great she looked nearly nude. But of course Quiti herself looked good, per one of the myriad gifts of the hair.

She had already lost the rotten tomato wager, but she was glad to join the fun. She waded to her waist, then held her breath, closed her eyes, and dropped the rest of herself into the sea.

Something was wrong. There was no water pressing against her face. She opened her eyes and discovered a translucent shield in front of her head, holding back the water. Her eyes were dry, and she could breathe.

Yet she really was under the surface. It was the hair, angling down from her forehead and forward from the sides, like the frame of a face mask. Not only did it keep the water at bay where it was, it seemed to project a field that blocked the water, letting only oxygen through. An effective gill.

She could breathe!

Amazed, she put her feet down and stood up, emerging from the water. Gena was there. "Quiti! Are you all right? You went under and didn't come up!"

"I am more than all right," Quiti said. "Gena, I can breathe underwater!"

"Without gills?"

"Yes. The hair is like an oxygen mask. I'll show you."

She descended again, and Gena went with her, watching closely. The woman slowly poked a finger through the glass-like field. It did not pop; it simply surrounded the finger, sealing to it.

Back above the surface, both of them were excited.

"You can't drown!" Gena said. "It repels the water, but lets you breathe. It's a chemical filter."

"I wonder how far it goes? Could I swim any distance underwater?"

"Let's find out, girl! If you were aboard a cruise ship and it sank, you'd sure want to know about this!"

"I sure would," Quiti agreed.

"We'll go out to deeper water. I'll swim on top, you swim below. If you have any trouble, grab me and I'll haul you back to shallow water."

They tried it. Quiti stroked strongly, having more than enough strength. She readily outdistanced her companion, and had to slow the pace. It seemed she could swim indefinitely in this manner.

"How well will you swim when your hair is full length?" Gena asked, awed.

"I hope to find out."

They were now a fair distance out from the beach. "Uh-oh," Gena said.

"What?"

"I see a fin."

"A fin?"

"There's a shark circling us."

Quiti felt a chill. "We can't out-swim that."

"We can't," Gena agreed. "And I left my knife behind."

What to do? "I can make my skin hard. Maybe too hard even for that to bite."

"What if you're wrong?"

"Maybe I can reach its mind. Stay behind me. I mean, so I'm between you and it."

"Quiti, you've got no call to sacrifice yourself!"

"I'm not. The hair's not afraid, so neither am I." Quiti oriented on the circling fin, then swam directly toward it. *Go away, fish-face, before you annoy me,* she thought at it.

The shark actually looked startled. Then it turned tail,

literally, and fled.

"But let's not push our luck," Gena said, and stroked for the shore.

Quiti followed, relieved.

Then she saw the fin again, this time heading directly for Gena.

"You bastard!" Quiti swore. She doubled her stroke, accelerating at a rate that surprised her, and swam to intercept the shark. She grabbed at its tail.

The shark whipped its head back to bite her. This time she punched it in the snoot. It was no token blow; she felt the cartilage of the shark's face crushing under the impact. It was hurting. Again it fled.

This time it did not return.

"I saw that," Gena said. "You punched it out."

"It annoyed me. I had warned it."

"I guess you did. You are one tough girl."

So it seemed.

They left the water, showered in the facility to get the salt and sand off, and returned to the rig. "For some reason I am no longer as keen on swimming as I was," Quiti said.

"Me neither. Can't think why."

Gena found a citrus fruit load to haul to Oklahoma. Her rig was not refrigerated, but ice would suffice for this if they didn't dally. She got loaded and they set off.

The first night out they had to park near a forest. As they remained parked, Quiti perked up her head. "I smell a shark fin."

"Your hair's alert," Gena said. "Out here there's a small chance it could be marauding bears, and a big chance it could be men."

Quiti turned her head. "Men. They've got us surrounded. Maybe six of them. I think they know we're young women; the sex on their minds is coming through strongly."

"Okay, we've got maybe three choices," Gena said.

"One is to crank up the rig and hightail it out of here right now."

"And maybe run a couple of them over in the process," Quiti said. "That would be manslaughter. I'm not up to it. They—their minds indicate they're not bad men, just hot for sex. They actually think women say no just for appearances; that they really want it just as much as the men do. They're in denial, at least about sex."

"A chronic state, with men."

"Damned if I want to say no no and have them hear yes yes."

"Two: give it to them, so they'll go away. I could do it while you hide."

Six lusty men? Quiti continued to pick up on the surrounding minds. "They know there are two of us, and I'm the one they want more."

"Three: use one of your tricks to scare them off."

Quiti smiled. "I think that will do."

They quickly rehearsed their plan. Then they got out of the truck, leaving its parking lights on so that they could be seen. More important, so that the men closing in on them could also be seen. Quiti oriented on each in turn, planting subtle effects.

The men came, surrounding the cab. "Hi there, sweethearts!" one called. "Looking for a good time?"

"Maybe," Gena said. "Come a little closer, dearies, so we can see what you've got."

"We've got this," the man said, opening his pants to reveal a standing erection.

Gena glanced at Quiti. "What do you think? Will he do?"

"He looks full of blood."

"Let's get out of these confining clothes. Can't vamp properly in them."

They quickly stripped naked, knowing the effect it

was having on the men. Their minds were wide open to suggestion.

"Are we ready to vamp, sister?" Gena asked Quiti.

"More than ready. I'm hungry as hell."

"Then let's feast tonight!"

The men were so eager they were practically drooling. Now they all had their members out.

Quiti let loose with her illusions. Suddenly the two women were sprouting fangs and wings.

"Vampires!" a man exclaimed.

"Vamps," Gena agreed. "Let me at you, you luscious piece of meat!"

The two women advanced on the men. The men retreated.

"Don't let them get away!" Gena said. "We can have three apiece. That much blood will hold us for a month."

But the men were already fleeing.

"Come back!" Quiti called. "Only the first bite hurts!"

Their pleas were of no avail. The men were gone.

Gena and Quiti hugged each other, laughing.

"That was so much fun," Gena said. "I could almost see your fangs and wings myself."

They returned to the rig and dressed, knowing the men would not be back.

They delivered the citrus fruit without further event, found another load, and drove on west. There was no further question of their continued association; they liked each other and were having a ball.

Two weeks later they were back in California. Quiti's hair was now close to six inches long, and her powers were still increasing. "Now you get to meet Idola," Gena said.

"Is this wise? I don't want to complicate your relationship."

"I'll want to meet your family, too, some day, when you're no longer on the lam."

They took nine year old Idola out to an amusement park. She was brown haired and brown eyed, like her mother, and seemed fated to be as lovely as an adult. She was shy about meeting Quiti.

"Touch her hair, dear," Gena said.

The girl did. "You're telepathic!" she said.

The hair was becoming too expressive for Quiti's complete comfort. "It may only seem that way."

"And I won't tell," Idola said. "I like you."

"I'm glad."

"Will you teach me how to read minds?"

"That's not something I can do," Quiti said.

"Oh, yes, it's the hair. I wish I had hair like that."

"Yours is lovely as it is," Quiti assured her.

"But it can't read minds."

"It can't read minds," Quiti agreed.

They had a fine afternoon, and Quiti did enjoy it and the girl's company. By the end of the day she was quite satisfied to be a peripheral part of Gina's larger family. She was becoming Auntie Quiti.

Meanwhile they continued to explore the developing powers of the hair. When they had time alone, they tried jumping off a rising wall, at first from a low level, then higher. The hair flared out like a little parachute, and really did seem to slow her descent.

"I think more is going on than just parachuting," Gena said. "You're falling too slow."

"I felt light," Quiti agreed. "But I can't feature antigravity."

"We'd better find out, all the same. As your hair grows, it seems to be developing new qualities as well as strengthening the old ones. We need to know what they are."

Quiti could only agree. She went to the highest section of the wall, then jumped down about five feet, bracing for a hard impact. But the hair flared and took hold, and lifted her by the head, so that the impact was soft.

"How far does it go?" Quiti asked rhetorically.

"This makes me nervous, but we still need to know."

They considered. Then they gathered fallen leaves to make a pile under a spreading oak tree, and Quiti climbed up the trunk with surprising alacrity, hung from a branch, and dropped about seven feet onto the pile.

The landing was soft. This time there was no doubt that the hair was holding her up to a degree, so that her fall was slower than it should have been.

She climbed the tree again. This time she stood on the branch, making her descent about twelve feet. She jumped.

And the landing was no harder than before.

"It's more than parachuting," Quiti said. "I'd need a full sized parachute to slow me this much, rather than an eighteen inch flair."

"Do you have an invisible jet motor?"

"I don't feel any jet passing my face."

"Maybe magnetic repulsion of the ground?"

"Maybe," Quiti agreed dubiously.

"We need smoke or vapor, so we can see what the air is doing around your hair."

They went to a pond and Quiti focused on vapor. Her hair reached toward the water. Suddenly there was visible vapor rising, forming a thick fog. It expanded and drifted over the pond and adjacent ground. Just what they needed. But now they were away from the tree.

Impatient, Quiti tossed off her clothes. "Lift me up. Tell me what you see."

Gena bent down, caught hold of Quiti's legs, and heaved her up. Then Quiti jumped down through the patch of fog.

"There was a swirl of air going in toward your head," Gena reported. "And another swirl going down, and some up. But no single direction. It's not making sense to me."

"Yet it is somehow lifting me."

They continued experimenting and discussing it, and concluded that it was a combination of effects: some magnetic repulsion, some antigravity, some jet propulsion. That it in effect subtracted about fifty pounds from her weight, so that she fell more slowly and landed with less impact. The special fields were limited so that there was not the dangerous phenomenon that straight antigravity would cause: air without weight being squeezed out in a column as the pressure of the atmosphere pressed in, and forming a violent jet that would deplete all air in the vicinity. No, this ended a few inches away from the hair, so that the jet soon dissipated. The hair, or maybe the aliens who had cultured it, knew what it was doing.

However, that jet could be adjusted. Quiti learned how to angle her head toward standing water, and form it into a fire-hose blast that could devastate whatever stood before it. In short, it was a kind of weapon.

"Where is the limit?" Gena asked. "Suppose your hair grows to be five or six feet long? Will you be able to fly?"

"Yes." Then, hearing herself, she realized that the hair had given her the answer.

When Quiti mentally called Speedo that evening, he had news for her. They couldn't have a dialogue, though that might come as the hair grew, but she could read his most superficial thoughts as she zeroed in on him.

*They know where you are. They're watching you.*

Quite paused, mentally. How could he know that? He couldn't tell her, but he was sure. So she sent her message: *Thanks. I'll be alert. Tell my folks I'm fine.*

Then she talked with Gena. "Speedo says they're watching me. I don't know how he knows."

"Your eatery man. Try him."

Quiti searched for Joe's mind. Sure enough, he had a surface message for her. *Rumor that they've spotted the magic girl riding with a trucker.*

So he was the one who had told Speedo. Joe knew just about everything that went on in his neighborhood, because his hearing was better than his diners realized. *Hairpower here. Thanks, Joe.*

So now her friends back home knew that she knew. But what should she do? She didn't like being vulnerable. The authorities could close in at any time, and she'd have trouble escaping if they knew what she could do, as they surely did. Unless they underestimated her.

"If they know, and it sure seems they do," Gena said, "Why haven't they moved in on you?"

Quiti applied her enhanced brain to that specific problem, and the right question produced the answer immediately. "Because they've caught on that my hair gives me special powers. Those powers are more important to them than I am. They are letting me discover them myself. Once I am complete, probably when the hair is full length, they'll snap the trap shut."

"So maybe you're not threatened right now," Gena said. "But you will be when? In a year?"

"About then," Quiti agreed.

"So let's enjoy the year, traveling the country, as if we have no inkling. But you need to figure out how to disappear again when you need to. I'll be sad to see you go, in fact I'll be grief stricken, but it probably has to be."

Quiti hugged her.

They set off with a load for a town in Maine. When they were safely on the road, they talked. "I'm assuming that they can't bug us here on the moving truck," Quiti said. "That it's mainly that they spotted me on a surveillance camera and a computer identified me, so now they're tracking the rig. *Laissez-faire* surveillance. That's why the hair didn't spot it."

"They're getting smarter," Gena agreed. "They know that if they try to nab you, not only will you likely escape, but even if they get you, you won't cooperate, and they'll never see your full powers. They probably also want to know how you got the hair, and you'll never tell them unless they make real nice to you."

"They're not the enemy. It's their ignorance I fear. Maybe when I have full telepathy and can read their minds, I'll be ready to trust them."

"Maybe," Gena agreed again, as much with her doubt as with her words.

"But I do mean to be sure they can't hold me against my will. I need to be able to drop off their screen at any time."

"Your invisible head routine. When your hair is six feet long, you'll make your whole body invisible."

"To all wavelengths," Quiti said. "So their sensors can't pick me up. Vision, sound, radar, heat, everything."

"Everything."

≈≈≈

A year passed, mostly on the road. Quiti kept in touch with Speedo, Joe, and thus her family. Meanwhile her hair grew. When it reached her waist, she gave up wearing a regular shirt or bra; the hair did the covering and her breasts needed no support whatever. The hair was on the way to becoming an encompassing cloak that never needed combing or washing, and that would weigh about twenty pounds complete. The same as the original hairball.

When it reached her knees, she discovered further properties. It could emulate her clothing, right down to the buttons and belt. It also insulated her body, maintaining comfortable temperature and humidity. Not only could she wear it instead of her clothing, it was better than clothing. She gave up clothing entirely, including underwear, carrying her wallet in a loop the hair obligingly made. The hair had become her blouse, skirt, and even her shoes as it curled under her feet. It looked exactly like regular clothing, and she changed its appearance daily so there would be no suspicion. It even emulated shorter regular hair, the pattern of brown curls around her shoulders, or a braid down her back. Hair imitating hair!

"I envy you," Gena said. "No fuss, no muss, no laundry. You never get sweaty or cold. It never chafes. It's always in style. And it's about as cheap as you can get."

"I don't yet know what the hairballs will require. It was presented as a return favor, but I suspect it was more like a consignment. There has to be much more of a price to pay, when it finally comes due."

"Get real, girl! Without it you'd be six months dead by now."

"True." Because it was now absolutely clear that her cancer was gone.

More, they discovered that it protected her. They experimented, with Gena first striking with her fists and encountering only gentle but effective resistance, then with a hammer, then stabbing with a large heavy screwdriver. Nothing got through.

They got more experimental. Gina hosed water on Quiti, and it simply washed off without wetting her. She got a blowtorch, and the hair did not even shrivel, it merely dampened out the flame. Finally, nervously, Gena tried a pistol she kept for emergencies, firing at the fringe so that Quiti would not be hurt if the hair failed. But the bullet dropped to the ground, neither Quiti nor the bullet itself harmed. Her hair skirt was truly invulnerable.

It also could emit gases, including ones that would put other people to sleep. That could be useful if a crowd ever attacked her. But that was dangerous, because too much of it could kill people. She would use it only if the situation were dire and there seemed to be no alternative.

But mainly they worked on the flying. Idola was desperate to participate, and could be trusted, so they took her out one day for a long forest hike, got alone, and practiced levitation. When Quiti focused, the hair blew out in a cone starting at her head and extending to her feet. Air circulated and she lifted off the ground, her body within the cone like the clapper of a bell.

Idola, now age ten, was delighted. "Hair skirt!" she cried, pointing upward. "And your panties are showing!"

"I'm not wearing any," Quiti called down.

"Yes you are. I see them."

Quiti felt a curl of the hair in that region. A lock of it was giving her the illusion of panties, to keep her respectable. That was probably just as well, though she had no intention of flying in public.

Navigation remained tricky. It required mental nuances to angle the gravity jets properly, so that she could not only lift vertically but also propel horizontally. Slowly she trained herself, so that she could fly with increasing precision.

"Good job," Gena said, satisfied. "You'll never fall down a well and get stuck."

"I wish I had hair like that," Idola said.

"Don't we all," Gena said. "But Quiti's one of a kind."

Now the hair was as long as she was, and her powers were still being explored. They knew the authorities would not wait much longer to grasp what they thought was theirs.

The last thing they worked on was the telepathy. Quiti could now contact Speedo at any time, and dialogue with him. But the one she most wanted to be mentally close to was Gena. "As far as we know, they can't yet detect telepathy," Quiti said. "So we can remain in touch regardless of physical proximity."

"I want that. Quiti, you're the very best thing that's happened to me, and I don't ever want to lose you."

"With the telepathy, we'll never be far apart."

"I count on that."

"You have enabled me to grow the hair to full length.

I sincerely appreciate that. But I have also really enjoyed being with you."

"Double ditto here! I'm bound to be lonely, driving alone, when I never was before. Just bored."

"Maybe you should retire from driving and find a good man."

"Maybe I should. But I won't. Garden variety life has lost its appeal. I'll wait for your thought, and wish I could meet a hairball like yours."

"I fear the next tour will be our last together. They are getting ready to pounce. I feel the background tension."

"We know what to do when they strike."

They hugged. Then they boarded the rig.

They were hardly a hundred miles on their way when Quiti felt it. "The trolls are gathering," she reported.

Gena kept her eye on the road. "We knew they would. We're as ready as we'll ever be."

Quiti ranged out with her mind in a manner she had been able to do only recently; before, it had been only the hair doing it. "It seems they want to intercept us on the road, in anonymous country, so that there are no witnesses to my disappearance. So there will be no newspaper reports of any missing person, no hue and cry. No speculation about magic girls. I think that's another reason they waited: as long as I was away from home, not in contact with my folks as far as they knew, no one should notice."

"Do you have a better idea what they really want with you?"

"To virtually take me apart in the laboratory, examine every follicle of my hair, find out exactly what it is and how it works. Subject it to chemical and fire testing to destruction. They don't know about the hairball; they think it's a very special mutation, maybe sponsored by the cancer. A cure for cancer is the least of their aspirations."

"And they don't know the quarter of it."

"They don't. And I am not going to let them find out. Not yet. Not until I know more about the hairballs."

"Plural?"

"I met only one, but he had to be a member of an alien species. I want to visit his flying saucer ship, or whatever, and learn why he contacted me."

"Because you were a good person."

"Because I sought to help a creature in evident need," Quiti agreed. "Instead, he helped me. But I just don't believe in decency or compassion with respect to interstellar alien species. There has to be a more practical reason. I want to know it."

"More power to you, girl."

"They are closing in. Gena, don't stop, even if they try to flag you down."

The woman laughed. "I know my role. Don't worry. I won't stop until it's too late for them."

"Thanks." Quiti leaned across and kissed her on the cheek. "Farewell."

"You too," Gena said tightly. Quiti saw that there was a tear in her eye.

Then she accelerated, swinging through the turns at dangerous velocity. No one was going to catch her, let alone pull alongside her, let alone halt her.

Quiti wound down the window and set herself before it. Then she plunged out, her hair going conical as she took to the air. She flew, then faded to invisibility and hovered high enough to watch the action.

The rig zoomed on. Right behind it came the pursuit car and several others. They could take the turns more readily than the big truck could, but they could not pass it. Then there came a straightaway and they pulled up, honking and flashing lights.

The rig slowed but did not stop. It cruised on several more miles before finally yielding to the imperative of the cars and grinding to a halt beside the road. Men piled out, surrounding it, and these ones plainly were not looking for sex.

And of course all they found was an irate female driver, demanding to know what the sam hell they were bugging her for?! She had a load to haul.

Quiti smiled, invisibly. The trap had sprung, but missed the mouse.

# CHAPTER 7:
## *Roque*

Quiti flew to the ground, resumed physical visibility only, reset her clothing and appearance to something completely different from her norm, and walked to a nearby restaurant she had spied from the air. Now she resembled a tired older woman with spectacles and too prominent a behind.

She was in luck. There was an all you can eat entree. She took it, piled her plate modestly, but then went back twice more when others weren't watching. She got a good bellyful.

It was still morning. She made sure no one was watching, then shifted to a new aspect: a young man roughly resembling Speedo. She got beside the highway and put out her thumb. Her mind was questing to be sure there was no dangerous driver in the vicinity. She was looking for a ride to take to a freight train stop about twenty miles distant. The train was going in a direction she wanted: where there was mental wind of a man. Would it work out? From this distance she could not be sure, but there was definite hope.

She was picked up, to her surprise, by a woman. She hesitated. "You sure, ma-am?"

"Get in, sonny. I've got a son like you."

Oh. Quiti got into the car.

"Actually I had a son like you," the woman said as she

drove. "He's dead. I miss him."

"I'm sorry. If I may ask—?"

"Cancer. Melanoma. We thought the skin tumor wasn't serious. Until it metastasized."

This hit Quiti where she lived. "I—I know about cancer. My—my sister had it. Brain cancer. Inoperable. She's gone now."

"Maybe I knew it. There's something about you that shows it."

Quiti realized that that something might have been her mind questing out, intersecting the woman's mind. Sometimes a person was aware. The woman had picked right up on that aspect, attuned to it. "It's awful."

"Where you going?"

"To the freight stop. Thought I'd hop a train."

"My son did that. It's illegal, you know."

"I know. But affordable."

"That's how he saw it."

"I think I would have liked him."

The woman drove her to the stop. "Take care of yourself."

"I will. Thanks."

It was several hours before a train came. Quiti settled down against a wall and contacted Gena. *Hairpower here. You okay?*

*Lonely.*

*So am I. I'm sorry. I'm waiting to catch a freight train.*

*Where are you going? No, cancel that; I don't want to know anything that might mess you up.*

*This is okay. I've got mental wind of a man like me. With hair.*

*Oh, Quiti, I hope you find him.*

*I hope so too. I'll be in touch again.*

Then she contacted Speedo, letting him know that she was no longer with the trucker. *I'm off their screen, I trust.*

*I hope. You'll always be on my screen.*

She laughed mentally. *Remember: get yourself a girl. Not with hair like mine.*

*Got any in mind?*

*No. The ones I know are too old for you, or too young.*

*I'm at an awkward age.*

*Wait another year.* She faded out of sight and napped.

The train came. While it was being re-tracked for its destination, she quietly climbed onto a car, up it, and settled on the roof. Her hair spread out and anchored her there, happy to be in the glare of the sun. None of the inordinate heat of it touched her body. She slept.

A thousand miles along, at night, she got off the train. There were no restaurants handy, and she was hungry. The hair still needed physical sustenance. She went to a grocery store and bought a bag full of turnips. Then she got private and ate them all.

Now she oriented on the man she was tracking. He was a hair suit! About six months behind her, on the hair, which was most of what counted. Now he was approximately ten miles away.

This time there was a bus going that way. She took it, now back as a young but not too attractive woman. Attraction was deadly when the object was to be unnoticed.

She got off two blocks from the man. This was a loading dock area, the kind she had encountered often enough when riding with Gena. He was a worker there.

She followed his mind with increasing definition, liking what she found. He had had a vaguely bad background, but the hair had changed him completely, and now he was a good man. Her man.

She halted near the dock where he worked. She watched him loading bales of clothing. He stood about five eleven, had nice musculature, and green eyes like hers. He would do, physically. Not that it mattered; what counted was the hair.

She sent him a thought. *Hairpower.*

Startled, he looked her way. He read her mind, which she had on display for him. *We'll marry next month.*

*Of course.*

Then she went to him and sealed it with a kiss.

She waited while he completed loading the truck, checked out, and went home, theoretically alone, as she arranged to be visible only to him. Then, secure in his spare apartment, they communed mentally, as only two hair brained people could. She gave him her history and he gave her his.

Roque was just 18 when his parents died in a car crash. The cause was unknown; there was no alcohol or drug residue in either of them. The vehicle had suddenly veered and crashed into a concrete bridge pylon, killing them instantly.

He had a fair guess why. Their marriage had lasted 21 years but was in trouble. Each had cheated on the other, and each blamed the other. They planned to divorce the moment they could afford to. They had argued constantly. They must have had a bad tiff in the car, weakened focus at a key moment, and lost control. He was shocked and grieved by their deaths, but most of what he had wanted was to get out of that house and on his own, to be free of the deadly tension. Now, abruptly, that had happened.

There was no money; their house had been underwater, owing more than it was worth, which was one reason they could neither sell it nor afford the divorce. Roque had no inheritance. He would have to try to get a job and survive, somehow.

Then his wealthy uncle Burke had stepped in. The man had never been close to the family, but felt obliged to see that Roque got a fair chance at his own life. He did not want to take in the surly teen, nor support him in an unsupervised life style. So he proffered a deal: go to college, work toward his degree, any degree, and Burke would support him as long as he maintained a passing average. Once he had his degree he would be on his own, but equipped for it.

Roque accepted the deal. He didn't want to move in with his uncle any more than the uncle wanted him there. So he rented a cheap apartment near the campus, whose minimal rent Burke also covered, and walked to classes. His tight allowance also covered his food. The uncle was ungenerous but fair; it was enough. In fact, batching it like this worked; it was getting him there.

He was not really college material, but he applied himself, studying hard. He was tall and lean, but no athlete, and girls his age simply weren't much interested in a car-less nobody, so he had time, to his deep regret. He dreamed of finding a pretty girl who liked him for himself, but knew that wouldn't happen until he had his degree and a good-paying job. He got by generally with C grades. He made it through his freshman year, and his sophomore, unspectacular but steady.

In his third year luck struck. A luscious-looking woman his age hailed him as he walked to the campus. "Looking for a good time, handsome?"

Oh. A prostitute. No other girl would call him that. "I'd love to get laid by a creature like you," he said. "But I lack the money. I don't even have lunch money; I eat at home, and bring a sandwich."

She did not move on immediately. "I've seen you around, hoofing it to the campus. You don't seem to drink or gamble or eat fattening foods. You live with your folks while you go to college? I envy you."

"No folks. They're dead. I'm batching it alone."

"Oh. Too bad. At least you're smart enough to make it on your own. I'm not."

"But aren't you a——?"

"A whore. That's what I mean. If I were smart, I'd go to college too, and make something of myself. As it is, all I've got is my body. When that wears out, I'm done for. My pimp abused me and took most of what I earned. I'd dump it all in a moment if I had any choice."

This was curious. "He doesn't abuse you anymore?"

"He ran afoul of a mobster and got rubbed out yesterday. So I'm between pimps. The next one will probably be worse."

"A beautiful creature like you," he said in wonder. "I thought all, um ladies of the evening were well off."

She laughed. "No. We're mostly dirt poor. That so-called beauty is mostly lean times and a push-up bra. At least I'm not on drugs, yet."

Why was she talking to him? "I guess you're worse off than I am, then. I'm sorry."

"Listen, you seem like a good kid, not the kind I deal with every night. I need a place to crash days. Maybe this is my chance to make it on my own. How about a deal: let me use your place, and I'll guarantee you sexual satisfaction from three AM to seven AM every morning. I won't mess up your apartment. I'll even kick in some cash toward the rent. I won't bring in any johns. What do you say?"

This was more than interesting. "Where's the catch?"

"Maybe it's that you'll be wasting your time, apart from the sex. I'm not relationship material. I'll never be your girlfriend. We can't be seen together outside. And one day I'll be gone, either killed on the street, abducted by a mob, or arrested. When it happens, don't try to locate me. Just accept that it's over."

Roque nodded. "It certainly isn't perfect, but it will do. What's your name?"

"Desiree. That's my stage name. You're better off not knowing my original name."

"Roque." He hesitated. "Are you sure you want to do

this?"

"I see you need persuading. Okay, here's a sample." She put her back to a telephone pole, spread her legs, and hitched up her skirt. She wore no panties. "Put it in, soldier."

He stood before her, but couldn't act, daunted. He had never actually had sex with a woman before. "Uh—"

"Like this." She reached for him, opened his fly, brought out his stiff member, and put it to her crotch. She actually produced a condom and efficiently put it on him. "Bend your knees, get down a little, then push up from below." She lifted to her tiptoes.

He followed her instructions, while she kept her hand on his member, guiding it in and settling her body around it, and in moments he was pulsing into her. "Oh!" It was all he could manage to say at the moment.

"See? All done." She removed the condom and put his spent member away. "But it's better naked. See you in the morning."

"Uh, here's a duplicate key." He detached it and handed it to her, then gave her the address.

"How sweet. I'll be there."

They separated, he going to his classes, she to parts unknown. He was in a daze. Would she really come next day?

She did, at three in the morning, as promised. She had a suitcase, which she set down. "Let me use your bathroom to clean up, then I'll be with you."

Roque waited awkwardly. He remained uncertain this was wise, on his part, but the temptation of easy, competent sex was overwhelming.

Soon she emerged, splendidly naked. She did have the figure, push-up bra or no. "Get your clothes off, Roque. We've got things to do."

He stripped, then joined her on the bed. She conjured a condom from somewhere and got it quickly on him, then clasped him and drew him in for another instant climax.

"You're right!" he gasped. "It's better naked."

"Now I will do what I seldom do: I will remain to enjoy your company."

Encouraged by her, he soon found himself telling her about his situation, the death of his parents, the somewhat stingy largess of his uncle. He didn't even notice that she was sharing none of her own background.

Then she had him lie on his back, and she bestrode him. "Feel my boobs," she said, taking his hands and putting them on her breasts.

His limp penis quickly thickened and stiffened again. She got another condom. "Always use protection," she said. "You don't know where I've been or what I've been exposed to. Assume the worst." She lifted her torso, took his sheathed member, and held it in place as she descended on it. He saw it going into her vagina, and was so excited he climaxed almost before the penetration was complete. Then she lay on him and kissed him. "There's more, but there's no hurry."

They talked some more. After a while she kneeled beside him, put her head down, and took his member into her mouth. She licked and gently sucked, and before long his penis was spouting again.

"That's oral," she said.

He simply lay there and savored the moment.

A while later she had him lie behind her, cupping her body, and fed his member in to her vagina from that side. Soon he was thrusting and into his fourth orgasm. Each one was different, unique to itself. "Oh, Desiree!" he breathed.

She got up and went to the bathroom. "That's how it'll be every morning, if you want it, or any other way you want. But then you have to let me sleep. I've had a hard night's work."

"I don't think I could do another anyway."

"Oh, you could if I made you. But why push it? I'll be

here tomorrow."

He got up, dressed, and fixed a breakfast of waffles for them both. She ate appreciatively. Then she handed him a twenty dollar bill. "Buy some eggs and bacon. We'll have them tonight before I go out to work."

He left for his classes, seeing her lying down alone on his bed. Would she really be there when he returned?

She was, and she fixed the bacon and eggs for them both. Then she went out, leaving him to do his homework, watch TV, and sleep.

At three in the morning she was back, her night done, using his key to let herself quietly in. He had remained awake late, too worked up to sleep, and so was asleep when she came. He woke to discover her beside him, naked. He clasped her, and climaxed in her, and returned to sleep in her embrace.

"Damn," she said when they both woke later. "Forgot the condom. You should remember it when I don't."

"So you won't get pregnant?"

"So you won't get an STD."

He didn't argue the case, but he wasn't always perfect about the condom.

So it continued. Roque was in a kind of heaven, loving not only the sex but the brief company. After the first day he was satisfied with a single sexual episode, followed by company at breakfast, which he liked almost as much.

"Don't get hooked on me," she reminded him. "I'm bad news, long term. Just enjoy the sex."

"Do—do you enjoy it too?"

She laughed. "Roque, sex is my business, not my pleasure. I like doing my job well."

"You don't climax?"

"I'll fake it for you, if you like, as I do with my johns."

"No! I want it real."

"I'll show you how to make me come. That's the best

I can do."

She did, guiding him in oral sex on her, and he found it fascinating to see her in the throes of her orgasm. But it remained only sex for her.

"Why do you stay with me?" he asked. "You're giving me so much, all this sex I could never afford, and money too. How can it be worth it to you?"

"It's the peace of mind, Roque. You're a good man, not the kind of prowler I screw with every night. I can sleep without being on guard against attack or robbery. I can leave my stuff here knowing you won't steal anything. You don't even look in it."

So she had her way of knowing. He never touched her things, honoring her privacy. "It's the least I can do."

"It's more than I'm used to. It makes me feel like I'm with a friend."

"We *are* friends, aren't we?"

"Come here, lover." She took him over and launched him into sexual heaven. It was her way of cutting short a dialogue she was not entirely easy with. She was not looking for friendship or romance, just temporary trust.

So it continued for six months. He made sure to maintain his grades, so that no one would suspect how his life had changed. So she was a prostitute; she was also a person, and he liked her, though he knew better than to say so. Did she like him in return? She never hinted at it, but that could be to keep him from getting any romantic ideas. He liked to think that she did.

Until the morning she did not appear. That suddenly it was over. He found it hard to accept, but he did what she had told him, and made no inquiry.

But as he walked to his classes, a stranger intercepted him. "Desiree got caught in a sting," she said. "It's not her first offense. She'll be years in prison. Throw out her stuff." She walked on.

It was evidently another prostitute who knew something of Desiree's business. Roque's emotions were mixed. He was glad that she had not simply deserted him, but sorry that she would be in prison.

Her suitcase remained in his apartment. He looked through it, finding only incidentals and one wallet-sized picture of an older couple. The woman faintly resembled Desiree: surely her mother, before she died. It was so sad.

He did throw out the other things, as there was no point in keeping them and they might be mischief if the police should track her and search his apartment. But he saved the picture, putting in his own wallet as a memoir. He owed her that much.

A month later he felt ill, and checked with the college infirmary. They took a blood test.

He had AIDS. There was no cure, merely palliative treatment to delay its progress.

Desiree hadn't told him, and he had never suspected. She had had more than one reason to discourage his long term interest. She had no long term to offer.

He couldn't condemn her. She had lived her life as well as she could, possibly in denial, pretending that she had a future. Maybe she had hoped that he would not catch the virus from her. He understood that it did not readily transmit. Maybe if they had had sex less often, he would not have. It had been a fair gamble.

And what was his own future now? What was the point in carrying on to get his degree, when he was unlikely to be able to use it gainfully?

Distraught, considering suicide, he walked the neighborhood. Was there a convenient place to end his life before it became unbearable? He had never been the suicidal type, but it might be the rational thing to do at this point.

He walked in a secluded park and stood by a pleasant little pond surrounded by statuary. He simply had no idea of his future.

*Greeting.*

He looked around, seeing no one. "I hear you, but can't see you," he said.

*I am here. On this head. I am hungry.*

Roque looked. What he had taken for a hat like a large anemone was actually a separate object, not part of the stone bust of a military hero. "You're telepathic!"

*I have no mouth and I must talk,* the thing agreed. *Feed me.*

Roque had no fear of the odd creature. "What do you eat?"

*Hair. Yours looks delicious.*

"Thank you. Take it; I think I won't be needing it long."

*Thank you.* The thing floated to him, landed on his head, and settled down. It weighed about twenty pounds, like a heavy helmet. He felt it consuming his hair. There was no pain or discomfort, merely that dissolving, as if he were undergoing a really thorough hair-wash. He still was not afraid or even nervous; he found this experience interesting.

Soon it was done feeding. It floated off his head. *Much appreciation; you have restored my vigor.*

"You're welcome." Roque could see in the pool reflection that he had become bald. "I guess you'll be on your way now, hairball."

*One thing. I must return the favor. What can I do for you?*

What was there to want, when he had no viable future? Then he thought of something. "If you have any such power, see if you can help Desiree. She's a good girl at heart, but she's dying too. I'd like to make her life easier, get her out of prison, with a regular job, maybe some faint hope for her future. This may be too much to ask."

*Will do.*

Roque was surprised. "This is possible?"

*It is a matter of influencing the right minds at the right time. Check her mind to verify it.*

"Check her mind? You forget I'm not telepathic."

*Not yet.* The hairball floated away.

Roque was left standing there, bemused. Had he imagined the whole incident? A graphic daydream? He put his hand to his head. His scalp was bare. Something had happened, maybe not exactly what he thought.

Regardless, he felt far more positive than he had when he entered the park. So he had AIDS; sometimes it went into remission. That could happen. Meanwhile he would make the most of whatever life he had remaining.

He did. He wore a cap to mask his sudden baldness and worked on his classes. They were easier to handle now, as if the coursework had gotten simpler, but he saw that his fellow students were struggling along much as before. When he turned in a paper and got his first A grade ever, he knew that something fundamental had changed. He hadn't even sweated the subject; he had just done what was required, and done it right.

That made him think, not about the academic subject but about himself. His life had changed far more dramatically than he had at first realized, when he encountered the hairball. He had become positive and smart, and his health was improving. His body was becoming steadily stronger and more handsome despite his baldness. And actually his hair was growing back, only not as it had been. It had been thick and brown; now it was as thick, but translucent, and lengthening at about six times the normal rate. He considered getting another blood test to check on the AIDS, but knew already that it would be either much reduced or gone, and that the test would attract immediate attention he preferred to avoid. So he didn't go, and he laid low in other respects too. He made sure he never got another grade A on a paper, though his mastery of the subjects had become a hundred percent. Let it be seen as a fluke. That was safer.

The hairball, in the guise of feeding on his hair, had

given him a remarkable gift, one he had not requested or expected. It had replaced his natural hair with a mat of fibers that acted to supercharge his brain. An almost literal thinking cap. As yet there seemed to be no end to it; the cap was growing and his powers were increasing. It was not entirely free; he had developed a ferocious appetite, consuming several times what he had before and never getting bloated or sick. He was, he realized, feeding the hair. So why had the hairball done this? Obviously it hadn't needed to feed on his hair; what it had was vastly superior. It had something larger in mind for him, and he was eager to discover what that might be. It must have been looking for someone with some potential, an amenable nature, and nothing to lose. He had obviously qualified.

He had told the hairball he was not telepathic, and the hairball had thought *not yet*. Now he understood what it had meant. Because he was slowly *becoming* telepathic. It was pacing the growth of his hair; the longer the hair, the more powerfully his brain performed, including mind reading. He could at first sense the moods of people nearest him, then some of their actual thoughts. Each day the ability grew stronger, and the range broader. He got so he could orient on particular minds at a distance, tracking them regardless where they went.

Then one day when his hair was three inches long he found the mind of Desiree. She was not in prison; she had been admitted to a special program to test a new drug that promised to put an AIDS victim into indefinite remission. Not a cure, but a suppression of the virus that might be almost as good. They needed years of tracking test subjects to ascertain the side effects, in case any were lethal, so there was risk. But hardly the risk of illness and death posed by the condition itself. She had been given a new identity in a program similar to Witness Protection, and had a legitimate clerical job and no pimps or johns. She was not supposed to contact anyone in her previous life, to prevent reversion; that was why she had not gotten in touch with him, to her regret. She was reasonably happy, and not just because of the prospect of living a longer life.

The hairball had come through.

Then Desiree felt his probing thought. *Roque! This is because of you!*

*Uh, no,* he thought, off-balanced by her discovery of his mental presence. *Not exactly.*

*You did it! You maybe cured me!*

*It wasn't me. But don't tell. I'm not supposed to be telepathic.*

*My thoughts are sealed.*

He was hugely relieved to have found her so well. But this could be awkward if she let anything slip.

*Don't worry, Roque,* she thought. *I owe you so much. I put you at risk for AIDS and didn't tell you, and now you helped me so much more than I ever deserved. You're such a great person. I had no idea you could read my mind! I'll never tell on you.*

Roque decided not to tell her that he had contracted AIDS, or about the hairball. *Thank you, Desiree.* He disconnected.

The hair continued to grow. He finished the college semester with carefully average grades, then took a summer job as a warehouse worker, moving heavy boxes and bales about. It was his way of exercising his new powerful muscles without attracting attention. He was now stronger than any athlete he knew, but as with the mind, he did not want to advertise it. He stayed strictly off the radar, knowing that if the phenomenal changes in him were generally known, his privacy would disappear. He wanted to give the hair time to grow as long as it was going to, and to do its thing, whatever that might be.

What was on the hairball's alien mind? There had to be a lot more than had shown so far. For one thing, was Roque the only human person seeded with the hair? His guess was there should be others, maybe some female.

And there was a hard-hitting thought. He knew now that the only woman for him would be a hairy one. One with looks, strength, genius, telepathy, and whatever, matching him. No ordinary girl would do, not because of lack of merit but because she would never understand his revised nature. So there had to be a super woman. How would he find her?

"And instead I found you," Quiti said. "My hair is a foot and a half longer than yours, so I'm more advanced. Smarter, stronger, more telepathic. But my logic is the same as yours: only a hair suit man will do for me, and in time you will surely match me. So shall I move in with you now? We have exchanged capsule histories, but there's a lot more catching up to do."

"I think not. Folk would notice if a lovely woman moved in with me. It was tricky enough when Desiree was here. We want to remain unnoticed until we decide on our future. We can associate unobtrusively by day."

"Then where will I stay?"

He considered briefly. "You might move in with Desiree instead."

She was taken aback. "The whore?"

He nodded. "If she's amenable."

"If *she's* amenable? What about me?"

"If you are the woman I know you are, you will work it out."

She gazed at him for a moment, working it out. "I will do it."

So it was decided.

# CHAPTER 8:
## *"Tillo"*

Quiti went to Desiree's apartment and knocked on the door. When the woman opened it, Quiti just stood there, thinking at her. *I am Quiti. I am Roque's woman. I have come to stay with you for a time until he and I marry. I am to be similarly secret, as you were when you stayed with him, but I will tell you whatever you wish to know and will help you when you need it.* The telepathy made it instantly intelligible and credible, and of course she had had the experience of Roque's telepathic contact.

Desiree gazed at her, astonished. "But I'm the whore!"

"You were the prostitute. You did what you had to do, to survive. It's a business like any other, providing a necessary service to society, regardless of the backwardness of the law. You made a deal with Roque, a fair exchange. He was more than satisfied."

Desiree smiled briefly. "I do know my business. But this is not something wives or fiancées understand. You should want to send me to hell, not room with me."

Quiti nodded. "I admit I was startled when he suggested it. But your deal was before I met him, and is in the past. I came to terms with it."

The woman didn't hesitate further. "Then welcome." Quiti knew from her mind that she felt as if she had known Quiti for years, and trusted her. Close mental contact could do that.

So it was that Quiti moved in with Desiree. That was no longer her name, of course, but it didn't matter; Quiti knew her as that from Roque's memory. In person she was a shapely blue-eyed blonde, not drop-dead gorgeous, but good enough to impress any man. Now she dressed conservatively, masking her assets; she was not much interested in attracting men at the moment. She was also a reasonably nice person, especially considering her background. Roque had lucked out when he encountered her; he could have done far worse.

Quiti sent her mental information about Roque's subsequent history and achievement of "magic" hair, and demonstrated some of what her own hair could do. Desiree was amazed to see her change her clothing without moving her hands or body, then make it transparent so she was effectively nude, and finally she disappeared entirely. "But I am still here," she said from the seeming space.

"Roque can do that?"

"Much of it. His hair is four feet long, compared to my five and a half feet, so it covers him less completely and has less power. But he will get there."

"I—about Roque—"

"He knows. He read your mind, remember? Your association with him was for mutual convenience, and you kept it carefully neutral. Of course he had a bit of a crush on you when you lived together; sex does that to a man. He still has a thing for you."

"After I gave him AIDS?"

Quiti nodded. "He knows you didn't mean to. That you tried to protect him from it. That if he hadn't pushed so hard he probably would have been spared it. So it was his fault as much as yours."

"And about the—the thing. I tried to hold him off emotionally. It was supposed to be just sex."

"You were upfront with him throughout, and he

appreciates that. His relationship with you has become more practical than sexual or romantic. Now he is mine."

"I see that. I'm glad for him. You are certainly the woman for him, and he's the man for you. But what *about* the AIDS? That's what I feel most guilty about."

"The hair abolished that first thing, just as it abolished my brain cancer."

"But there's no cure!"

Quiti smiled. "That's one of our secrets. The hair takes good care of us." She sent a mental signal that it was true.

"It sure does!"

"Now here's another example of its power."

This time she had her hair spread out into the cone that lifted her slowly from the floor. "That's right: I can fly. It also protects me from attack, whether by stone, knife, or bullet."

"But suppose they just grab onto you and don't let go?"

Quiti landed softly. "Touch my hair."

Desiree touched it with one finger. "Yow!"

"I charged it electrically, just enough to demonstrate. It's like touching an electrified fence. The power can be increased."

"No one will grab you," Desiree agreed, rubbing her hand.

"We have become very special people."

"But why? I mean, the hairballs—what do they want from you?"

"That is what we are waiting to find out. There has to be a price on this largess. Whatever it is, we'll gladly pay it. We have become creatures of the hair; it defines us and we'll do almost anything to keep it."

"Why are you telling me so much? I'd have let you be anonymous."

"We are special, but we do have to work with other folk. We can't see the future—that's one talent the hair does not bequeath—but you're a good person who knows Roque. You can keep a secret, and our association may continue some time. You need to know enough about us to judge whether that's something you really want."

"I already know I want it. Only—is that because you reached in and changed my mind?"

"Not directly. I am changing your mind by telling you about us. Informed consent is better than mind control."

"There's just something about you that makes me want to—to associate. If I were a man, I'd want to kiss you. I'll help you any way I can."

"For now, that means merely letting me sleep on your floor."

"The floor!"

"Remember, I can float. I don't need your bed. I just need to know I can relax without anybody messing with me."

"I know how that is," Desiree said reminiscently. "I must confess I did like Roque some, as I got to know him. He was so fair-minded."

"I won't be entering or departing visibly; no one else should know I'm here. I'm just camping while Roque completes his classes and gets his degree. Then we may both disappear from your life."

"I—I don't want that."

"We can stay in touch mentally if you wish."

"Yes! Roque has done me such a favor, getting me into this experimental program, maybe saving my life. It's more than I ever deserved. I'd do anything for him."

"You have done enough. But we'll let you know if anything else comes up."

Quiti settled in. Days passed. The world took no notice.

One thing did come up: their marriage. Roque was direct. "I want to marry you, as I said, and not just to have sex with you."

Quiti laughed. They had abstained from sex, sharing a certain reservation about the nature of their commitment.

"Ditto. Did you know I remain a virgin?"

"I know. It's too bad you didn't give it to that boy."

"Speedo. But I will give it to him once, when he's of age. I promised."

"He's almost of age now."

"When I see him again." She knew Roque would not be jealous. He had had his own experience.

"It will be an open marriage, in that respect."

"We can't have a formal public ceremony," Quiti said. "We don't want to get into the records. The powers that be would be on us in moments."

"True," he said thoughtfully. "But we do want to marry."

"We do."

"Maybe a small private—very private—ceremony, speaking our vows to each other, no witnesses, only ourselves."

"One witness," Quiti said. "Desiree."

He looked at her a moment. "You really have come to terms with her."

"I really have. I wrestled my mental state into shape. She's okay, and I like her. She knows us both, including how we are special. She will do."

"As you wish. It means I will be meeting her physically again."

"Do that. Hug her. Kiss her. Be her friend. She'll appreciate it."

"You're a wonder."

"I'm a hair suit." That said it all.

"You want me to what?" Desiree exclaimed, astounded.

"Witness our marriage," Quiti said. "You're my friend."

"But I can't see him again!"

"Why not? You're his friend too."

"You weren't fooling when you said you had come to

terms with what happened before."

"I'm not much for fooling," Quiti agreed.

Their agreed date arrived. Roque joined Quiti in Desiree's apartment. He really did hug and kiss her, chastely, and she actually blushed, distinctly not accustomed to such behavior. They sang the Hawaiian Wedding Song together, discovering that their ability was enhanced in this respect too: they had both become excellent singers.

Desiree even presented them with a small wedding cake she had bought. They exchanged glassy rings that were almost invisible, so as not to raise questions. They spoke their lines and kissed.

Then Roque's glance wandered to the bed.

"Take it!" Desiree said. "You're married, for Pete's sake. I'm going for a walk." She hastily departed.

They stripped and got on the bed, each brushing the long hair to the rear, where it still acted like a cloak. They did not need its protection from each other. "I'm depending on you to be competent," she told him, smiling. "It isn't as if you haven't been trained."

"Slow and easy the first time."

"What, no condom?"

He laughed. "We have no diseases, and you won't get pregnant unless you want to."

But when he made ready to enter, slow and easy, she grabbed him and pulled him violently in. Her vagina clamped hard on his member, milking it. Then a mutual orgasm was upon them, enhanced by their telepathic readings of each other's sensation. It lasted for several minutes. It seemed they were discovering yet another aspect of the hair. It really knew how to have a good time.

"Wow," she said as it finally eased. "I think I'm going to like sex, when we get better at it." As if it were possible to improve on their performance.

He laughed. "I'll try to do better. I felt the hair catching our emotional radiation and bouncing it back into us. I think it likes sex too."

"We got a lot of pleasure from such a simple act."

When Desiree returned after a suitable interval, she was amused. "You two should have damped your telepathy." They had remained tuned to her, in case she encountered anything they needed to know about, such as the janitor entering the apartment. "I might as well have been seated ringside at six inches distance with a huge magnifying glass. Sex sure isn't a dull business for *you*. I have to change my pants."

"Sorry about that," Roque said. But he was not *very* sorry.

Now Quiti spent her nights with Roque in his apartment, careful not to leave any evidence of her presence behind. By day she returned to Desiree's apartment, being similarly obscure. She had a fair amount of time to herself, and was bored. She mentally contacted Speedo and Gena, catching them up on her marriage. Then she thought of searching for other hair suits. She knew how to orient on Roque's mind, and adapted that to tune in on any hair-enhanced mind. And found none.

Well, maybe they weren't close by. She strengthened her focus and reached out ten miles, then a hundred miles, then a thousand miles, becoming excruciatingly finely tuned. The hair responded, tightening her focus. But there still was nothing.

Had the hairball enhanced only two people? It was possible, but seemed unlikely. At any rate, the survey was surely worth doing.

Day by day she reached out, changing her directional orientation slightly each time. She had the feeling that this was in accordance with the hairball's design.

Meanwhile Roque completed his courses and got his degree. He was in the lower half of his class, distinctly unspectacular by no accident. Now he could go out and seek gainful employment, the support of his uncle Burke ending. He moved out of his apartment and joined Quiti in Desiree's apartment; two could be as invisible as one. They were not in financial need; there were ways to unobtrusively make small amounts of money without attracting notice or cheating anyone, and they did. They would have contributed to the rent, but Desiree did not want to let any invisible income cast suspicion on her. She, also, was doing well; the experimental treatment was keeping her in remission and she was healthy in other respects.

Then Quiti got a nibble. Five hundred miles to the north there was a brain wave with incipient telepathy, typical of a hair suit.

Roque joined her, and together they amplified the signal. "Definitely something," he said. "Male."

"And young," she agreed. "A child."

"Um. Maybe we should stay clear, so as not to mess up his family situation."

"Maybe," she agreed. "But I am curious as hell. Could we go there and watch without contacting him?"

"Why not?"

"We're going to go check out a possible hair suit," they told Desiree. "We'll be back in a few days."

"Do come back," she replied. "I never had much of a social life before, and you guys are it, and I like it, even if no one else knows about it."

They caught a bus, traveling inconspicuously as a honeymooning couple. They reached the town and tuned in more competently. The person was indeed young and male, living with his large family in a tenement house, attending fifth grade classes in an inferior local school. He was indeed a hair suit; his hair was a yard long, covering two thirds of his small four and a half foot frame. He was by far the strongest and smartest of his classmates, but he had learned to hide his properties as well as his hair. His name was Tillo.

Again the question: should they communicate directly with the child? His situation seemed to be stable. All he needed was time to grow his hair to full length. That would be another year. They decided with regret to remain clear. Once Tillo had all his hair, they could reconsider. They caught the bus back.

A week later the situation changed dramatically. Tillo was in trouble, and suddenly confined in the children's ward of the local hospital for the criminally insane. What had happened?

"We've got to get him out, soon," Quiti said. "He belongs with us, not in that hellhole where they'll pull him apart trying to fathom what he is made of. They must already have an inkling."

Roque agreed. The boy's secrecy must have been breached. That was real mischief.

They hastily went to the local small airport and rented a plane and pilot to make the trip. They didn't have time or background for formal papers, so simply impressed on the pilot's mind their authenticity. This could be trouble if anyone thought to check on his business, but it was a risk they had to take.

Then they set up to spring the boy loose. But it would not be easy, as such hospitals were designed to be virtually escape proof. They formulated a plan and set about implementing it.

Meanwhile Quiti tuned in on the boy's mind, seeking his personal history. There might be information there that would help. She zeroed in on his encounter with the hairball the year before, which was prominent in his memories.

Tillo was not a popular boy, but they needed one more outfielder in their back-lot game, so he got to play, this one time. He had come out every day, hoping for just such a break, and finally it had come. So far he was doing okay; only one ball had come his way, dropping well short of his position, and he had fielded it and thrown it in. He had batted once and grounded out, a respectable performance considering his lack of experience.

Then a big boy hit a home run. It sailed over Tillo's head, out of the field, and through a window. The glass shattered.

Immediately the occupant, a florid middle aged man, charged out. The boys froze in place, knowing there really was no escape. "Who did that?" he demanded.

The team captain pointed to Tillo. "He did."

"Hey, wait!" Tillo protested. "I'm fielding, not hitting!"

"You hit it," the captain insisted.

"True?" the man demanded.

"It was him," the other players agreed.

Tillo realized he was screwed. They were lying to protect one of their own. The blame would stick, and his family would have to pay for the repair. His pa would take it out of his hide.

What could he do? He ran.

The others set out after him: the man and the players. Tillo realized as he ran that this must be the real reason they had let him play: to be the scapegoat if anything happened. That additional unfairness stung him worse yet. Nobody liked him; they just wanted to use him as a fall guy.

Tillo was no athlete, but one thing he could do was run. That came from being bullied by his siblings and peers. The easiest way to handle it was to get away from it. He remembered the saying that whoever said a person couldn't run from his problems never faced a bully. He had a good eye for deceptive escape routes, and he was familiar with this rundown neighborhood. He ducked into a dark narrow alley, dodged around a corner, angled into a darker alley, and dived under an empty crate. He pulled tattered newspaper over himself. They'd have trouble finding him, and if they did, he'd just run again.

The search passed him by. They never thought he'd stop running and hide. Soon the hue and cry was well beyond. Not that he'd really get away; they knew who he was, and would tell the occupant, who would demand payment from his father. That would in due course earn Tillo a hiding. He couldn't hide forever from the hiding.

So what was he to do? Run away from home? He'd be happy to leave it, but knew that the authorities would soon pick him up and return him there for punishment. If he did get away, where would he go? He knew some of the homeless folk of the neighborhood; bad as his life was, theirs was worse. He didn't want to join them.

He came out from the crate and looked around as if foolishly thinking there might be something there to save him. Like maybe a kindly rich old woman looking for a lost grand-kid to adopt and spoil endlessly. But there was nothing except discarded junk, including a yard-thick giant hairball that might have been a stage prop in a failed theater play.

*A greeting,* the hairball thought at him.

Tillo was not afraid of any hairball, because it lacked feet to run on and fists to strike with, but he was surprised. "That's you?"

*It is I,* the hairball agreed. *I need your help.*

Tillo laughed. "I can't help anyone. I'm hiding."

*Yes. You are good at hiding. I need to hide. Tell me how to do it.*

This was curious indeed. Tillo was flattered to have anyone or anything ask for his advice. "Well, first you have to do what they don't expect. Like not running far. Changing the way you look so they don't recognize you. Can you do that?"

*Perhaps.* The hairball shimmered and became another empty crate

"That's it!" Tillo exclaimed. "No one would know you for a giant hairball now. And you don't have to be a crate; you can be a brick wall, or a garbage can, or a leftover tire. Anything they don't expect and don't need. Then when they are gone, you can change back."

*I thank you, Tillo. You have been most kind.*

"You're welcome," he said, bemused that it knew his name. But it was telepathic, so must have pulled it from his mind.

*I must return the favor. What can I do for you?*

Tillo considered. "Can you make it so I don't get blamed for something I didn't do?"

*That is past remedying; the ill word has already been spread. But I can help you handle future situations in a superior manner.*

"Okay."

*I will need to take your hair.*

Tillo lifted his cap and considered his reddish mop in the dirty reflection of a piece of metal. "Okay."

The hairball floated toward him, then landed on his head. It was heavy, but Tillo was able to support its weight. Its body fastened on his head and did something.

Then it floated off. *It will take you time to learn the nuances, but they will come. Meanwhile proceed carefully.*

"Okay." The odd thing was that Tillo suddenly felt far more positive than he had until this moment. As if he could handle whatever came, no matter how bad. He had a better perspective. He put his cap back on what his brushing hand indicated was now his bald head.

*Until we meet again.* The hairball floated away and faded out.

"Bye," he called after it.

Okay, he was due for a hiding. But he could handle that; it was hardly the first time. His butt would be sore, but it was not the end of the world, or even his life. A week from now he would hardly remember it.

He went home, and it played out exactly as expected. His old man didn't even notice his loss of hair, partly concealed under the tight cap. Another odd thing was that it really didn't hurt as much as usual; it was as if his skin had toughened to handle it. But he hollered as loudly as ever it so it sounded as if he were really hurting. He was not a fool.

His sister Ilsa was home, a year his senior but not a bad sort. "Did you do it?" she asked privately. She knew about false blame.

"No. I was a patsy."

"You shouldn't try to play with those boys. They're bad news."

"I'll stay away from them after this. They'll have to find another patsy."

She wandered away, satisfied.

Then Tillo became aware of something new: he was hungry. In fact he was ravenous. Had the chase and punishment used up that much energy? This was a problem, because the family didn't have much food to pass around, and if he took more than his share he would be in instant trouble. He had to find food elsewhere. A lot of it.

What could he do? Compelled by the hunger, he went out into a nearby alley where filled garbage cans lined the narrow drive. He lifted the lid of the nearest. There was a plastic bowl of old chocolate pudding, probably way past its expiration date. But it made his mouth water. He dipped in a hand and scooped out a glob. He bought it to his face and licked it. It wasn't spoiled, just old. He gobbled it down, then licked off his coated hand.

He checked the next can. Nothing but old pillow stuffing there. He checked a third. It had a mess of old chicken bones. Okay. He chewed them carefully to be sure there were no sharp edges and swallowed them whole. He had never been partial to bones before, but now he loved them.

Soon he had a bellyful. He went home and lay down to rest and think. This new appetite was strange. Was it a fluke? Was it coincidence that it came so soon after his encounter with the hairball?

He had supper with the family as usual, as hungry as ever. He was required to remove his cap for the meal. That was when the others noticed his loss of hair. "Hey you got caught by the Shavers gang!" a brother chortled.

"I guess," Tillo said. The Shavers were a juvenile outfit that liked to catch unprotected boys and shave them bald. Small girls they merely depanted and looked at, as there tended to be too much of an uproar about their heads, and they normally did not talk about their embarrassment. Big girls remained well clear, knowing there were worse things than losing panties.

"Stay away from their territory," his mother said. "I thought you knew better."

"I will," Tillo promised. "I do."

But next day, hungry again, he found too little in the local garbage cans, and had to explore more widely. He drifted into Shaver territory—and got spied.

"Whatcha doing?" a big boy demanded, grabbing his arm.

"Nothing," Tillo said, mounting a surge of belief.

"Oh. Okay." The boy let go, and Tillo zipped away.

Then he paused to ponder. What had happened? Why had the boy taken his word? It was as if his push of belief had been effective.

Tillo was thinking far more carefully now than he had before encountering the hairball, and his belief in coincidence was nil. His mind felt supercharged.

He tested it on Ilsa. "Did the Shavers ever catch you?"

"Never!" she swore. But her mind had a memory, freshened by his query. They had caught her, taken her panties, held her legs apart, and taken a really good look.

They had even poked a couple of fingers in. She hadn't even dared scream, lest adult neighbors see.

"Are you sure?" he persisted, mentally pushing for the confession.

"Well, maybe they did, once. Don't tell."

"I won't."

So it was true. He could read a mind, and project a thought. It had to be because of the hairball.

After several days he noticed something else: his hair was growing rapidly back, but not as it had been. It was there, but transparent so that it did not show. Except that he could focus and change its color so it did appear.

He had another realization: it was the hair that made him so hungry. Not only that, but it wanted him out in the sunlight a lot. He took to sneaking up to the flat tenement roof, just so he could stand in the sun and feel the pleasure of his satisfied hair.

But his luck with the garbage cans ran out. One day he tripped an automatic sensor and it got a picture of him eating garbage. He couldn't mind-push that away. There was hell to pay. He had to stay inside the apartment except when accompanied by a parent or sibling, and neither type was pleased with the obligation. He wound up effectively locked in with Ilsa for hours at a time, as she was the one who disliked him least. She was satisfied to read a book, as they had no TV, as long as he didn't bother her.

But his hunger never eased. He had to eat, somehow. That was when his new mind developed another trick. It reached out and found the minds of vermin. They were simpler than human minds, and easier to influence. He pushed at the mind of a mouse and gave it the urge to come to their room. When it did, he grabbed it and bit its head off before consuming the rest of it.

"I saw that!" Ilsa said. "You ate a live mouse. You really are disgusting!"

"Don't tell," he said, chagrined to have been observed. He had thought she was absorbed with her reading, but she was cannier than he thought. He pushed at her with his mind.

"Stop that," she snapped, resisting him mentally. "I know you can read my mind; I've felt you before. Stay out of my head."

This was mischief. She knew too much about him, and had found a way to mentally resist him. He couldn't shut her up. He would have to make a deal. "What do you want?"

She smiled, victorious. "Two things. In return I'll do two things for you. I won't tell, and I'll help cover for you. Deal?"

"What two things from me?" he asked warily.

"First, tell me everything. I know something weird happened that changed you. Second, use your mind to make Parnell like me." She was in fifth grade; Parnell was a boy in seventh grade, handsome and articulate. She was as yet not developed, but boy-conscious, and working on a crush on him, though he didn't notice her.

"Deal," he agreed. Then he told her about the hairball, and his insatiable appetite. "So I've got to eat. Now I can't get at the garbage, so I'm summoning mice and maybe rats to eat. I don't care if they are alive; I just have to get that food into me. For the hair."

"How about bugs?" she asked, not disgusted now that she knew the story. "Teacher says there're more bugs in the world than anything else. That if you put all the elephants and things on a scale, and all the bugs on the other side of it, they would weigh more."

"Great idea!" he agreed. Then he proceeded to summon a rat, which he killed and ate. Then a slew of roaches, mosquitoes, ants, spiders, and wasps from outside.

"The way you gobble them down, you almost make me want to taste them," Ilsa said.

He laughed. "You can have any you want."

She grimaced. "I said almost."

Ilsa was true to her word. She kept watch when he was eating vermin and warned him when anybody was coming. When there was any suspicion of anything peculiar going on, she denied it. "We're just reading in here." The others thought maybe she was naughtily showing Tillo her panties or even her bare bottom, and sniggered, but had no inkling of the truth.

He in turn maneuvered to get close to Parnell, and engaged him briefly in mind-assisted dialogue. "You know my sister Ilsa's really not bad looking, and she likes you," he said, pushing belief. "She'd let you do a lot."

That was all it took: easy prey. Parnell oriented on Ilsa, and they became an informal couple. How much she let him do, especially as she developed, she didn't say, but she kept his attention. She knew what boys liked to see and touch. Tillo had completed his part of the deal.

Time passed. Tillo's hair grew, and with it his powers. He concealed them from others, deflecting their curiosity, and kept exploring and extending them. He became quite strong, but carefully gave way to bullies so they would not suspect. Similarly he became phenomenally smart, but didn't use it in his schoolwork. He had learned early the advantages of obscurity.

Until the day a year later. His hair was three feet long, and it protected him from any attack. But his interest was in whether it could enable him to fly. He really liked the idea of flying, though Ilsa cautioned him against it. "What you going to do, zoom through the air like Superman? They'd never leave you alone."

She was right. But the idea of flying had hold on his imagination. He knew that if he jumped down a distance, the hair flared out and slowed his fall. How far would it go? If he only had room enough, could he take off and fly? So he experimented cautiously. He went to the roof, as he often did so the hair could bathe in sunlight. Ilsa guarded the stairs; she would whistle if anyone else mounted them. The center of it was out of sight of the street and alley, so was essentially private.

It was a windy day, but that didn't stop him. He stood in the center, naked under the shroud of hair because clothing would only get in the way, spread the hair, and willed himself upward.

It worked! The hair formed a big cone that drew him up several feet, his own feet dangling.

A sudden gust of wind caught him and blew him to the edge of the roof, and over. He didn't fall, because he was still floating, but now he was several stories over the ground, instead of several feet. He tried to go back to the roof, but didn't know how to do a direction; he had not expected to move sideways. All he could do was descend under control, so as to reach the ground and walk back into the house.

But this was broad day, and there were people in the street. Dozens of them. They quickly spied him and stared up, amazed. He realized sickly that not only was he revealing his floating ability, they were looking up under the cone to see his bare legs and body. His privates. He couldn't close up the cone, because then he would plummet to the street, breaking bones if not killing himself.

Worse, some nut started shooting at him, as if he were a big bird to be hunted. This was a rough neighborhood; guns abounded, and were often enough used. The bullets bounced off the hair, but if that kept up, one would eventually come in under that cone and score on him.

There was a scuffle, and someone put the shooter out of commission. But someone must also have called 911, because there was a police siren approaching. Was he going to get arrested for disturbing the peace or something?

Finally he landed, and closed up the hair around him. But it was too late. The police were upon him. They caught him in a net so he couldn't fly away, and drew it tight so the hair could not flare into the cone. They tossed him into a van and hauled him away like some interesting trophy.

Now he was locked in a cell in the cellar of the hospital for the criminally insane. He read the closest minds to pick up on that. The reports that had been made of a naked flying boy were obviously crazy, and his exposure was obscene, so obviously this was where he belonged. It was a variant of the baseball frame-up, with him the fall guy again. He knew there would be no justice. He was doomed. All because of a stupid gust of wind!

The bars were tight, the gate locked. They knew how to keep a prisoner confined, in a place like this. He would never get out. His folks would disown him, rather than suffer another embarrassment. Even though there had been no direct, obvious examples, they knew there was something dangerously weird about him.

What could he do? Nothing but relax and wait for whatever was to come.

*There will be help.*

Tillo snapped alert. That was a telepathic voice!

Suddenly Tillo knew that things would work out. He relaxed.

# CHAPTER 9:
## *Hallelujah*

Quiti entered the hospital, nodding sociably as she passed the various guards and personnel. She reassured each that her presence was routine, that they knew her and trusted her, and she was legitimate. No one needed to see her papers or orders. She was just a visiting nurse who had come to see to the arrangements for the crazy wild child. That was just as well, because none of the regular personnel knew how to handle a naked boy who it seemed could fly. Not that they believed it for a moment. Still, it was awkward.

She was ushered down to the key cell. There was the boy huddled in the corner, not even using the bed.

*Tillo,* she thought. *Make no response to my thoughts, only to my spoken words. Trust me; I am your kind. The hospital personnel must not be allowed to know. I have come to take you away from all this, but you must cooperate with me.*

The boy did not move.

"Tillo," she said aloud.

Now he responded. "Who are you?"

"I am a nurse, come to see to your comfort. Look at me."

He looked. She flashed him with her body, showing the floor-length hair covering her nudity. This was not to impress him sexually, but to impress on him that she truly was his kind: telepathic with special hair.

*You are!* he thought gladly.

*I am. My name is Quiti, and I will be your guide out of hell.*

Aloud, she said "Come here, Tillo."

He came to the bars and stood, shivering with expectation. His kind!

Quiti turned to the accompanying guard and smiled, letting her beauty manifest. "Open the gate." When he hesitated, she applied some mental force. *It's the right thing to do.*

Obediently he brought out his key and unlocked it. He was a not completely unwilling slave to her will.

Quiti ushered Tillo out of the cell and the guard in. "You will remember none of this," she told him, touching his mind appropriately. "But you suspect that the prisoner mesmerized you. He's got weird powers."

She guided the boy up the stairs. *Keep mum. We're not out yet.*

They encountered a nurse in the hallway. "You see nothing," Quiti told her, verbally and mentally. The nurse walked on by, oblivious.

*You're good,* Tillo thought to her.

*I've had almost two years with hair.* They came in sight of the main entrance, but did not go there; there were too many people to handle cleanly. Instead they went up another flight.

But someone had caught on, at least to an extent; an alarm sounded. "Oh, hell!" Quiti swore. "I'll have to use the arsenal. Stay close."

Guards appeared, blocking off the upper hall at either end. Quiti could not cloud the minds of both contingents simultaneously, and didn't try. She focused on the man ahead. She caught his eye, then projected her holographic nude, which she had perfected in the last year. The apparition fairly scintillated, turning in place and smiling at the guard.

Tillo, checking the guard's mind, picked up on the nude.

*I'd sure like to have HER in my bed, when I'm grown,* he thought.

Quiti smiled. He was ten, but was a boy ever too young for a wicked peek?

The guard stood there, fascinated in more than one sense, as they walked right by him. They turned a corner, entering a new hall.

Another guard rounded the corner in pursuit. Quiti caught his eye and projected the alligator. The guard skidded to a halt, not about to tangle with such an ornery beast.

*You're doing tricks I never thought of,* Tillo though admiringly.

*I told you I'd get you safely out.*

The hall ended in a meeting room with a big picture window. Beyond it, outside the building, Roque hovered, tracking them.

"Wow!" Tillo breathed. "He can do it!"

Roque pointed to the side. There was a smaller access window, which he had opened.

*Take my hand.* Quiti took Tillo's hand. *We're going invisible, and flying away from here.*

*But I can't fly, really, just float. And I can't do invisible.*

*Then float. We'll do the rest.*

They climbed out the window. They spread their cones and hovered outside the building. Quiti steadied Tillo, and turned her hair invisible. *Follow my lead.*

And, tracking her mind, Tillo joined her in invisibility. This was not illusion; it was the hair concealing them both. "Wow!" he repeated appreciatively.

*Pull up your legs; they're showing.*

Oh. He hastily did so, and his exposed legs disappeared under his hair.

Roque took them both in tow, guiding them down to the street until they touched the pavement. There were people and vehicles, but though the flight stopped, the invisibility remained. Quiti and Roque walked closely on either side of Tillo, their hair spreading out to enclose his legs as well as their own. No one saw them.

They came to their hastily rented car. Roque drove while Quiti and Tillo rode beside him in the front seat, letting visibility return. "Contact Ilsa," she told Tillo. "Tell her you're safe with your own kind, and won't be returning. That she can have your stuff."

Tillo did so. His sister Ilsa was the only one he cared about. He was satisfied to leave his family behind.

"You'll have a new family," Quiti told him. "We'll be adopting you."

"Adopting?"

"I'm only twelve years older than you, but we're your kind. We hair suits have to stick together. You know that."

"I—I guess so." His mind was roiling.

"Anything else you need?" Quiti inquired.

"I'm hungry."

She reached into the back seat and hauled forth a quart container of high-protein nutritional drink. "We've got plenty more." She passed it to him, then got others for herself and Roque. "We know about hunger."

Tillo, overwhelmed by this understanding support, broke down and cried. Quiti put her arm around his shoulders, comforting him. He was a literal genius with a phenomenal body and phenomenal powers, but he was after all a child.

They drove home to Desiree, arriving the next day. She welcomed Tillo, recognizing the type, treating him like a little brother, and he was grateful for the non-judgmental association. This was a new role for her, too, but she clearly liked it. The three of them settled into her apartment, arranging to take up no more space than before, since they could sleep in a closet or in the air. Tillo got used to his new situation, and Quiti taught him new tricks with the hair. He learned rapidly, of course; he was hair smart, as were they, really beyond genius level, but there was much to master.

Roque and Quiti also continued to practice special effects, such as casting illusions and spot-controlling minds, knowing that they were likely to need them at some point in the future. They sang together, many popular tunes, enjoying the togetherness. It was a happy time.

One special project they worked on was what they called the Statue of Liberty ploy, wherein they sang "Battle Hymn of the Republic." They were perfecting it for a very special occasion, before a remarkable audience.

Two weeks later Desiree got bad news: the government drug study program she was in was being eliminated, a victim of budget cuts. She would have about two more months on the treatment; then it would end along with her job. She would be on her own. "This is senseless!" she railed, distraught. "The drug is working. It's almost a cure for AIDS. It'll do the world one huge favor when it is confirmed. How can they drop it now?"

"That is the nature of government programs," Roque said. "They come and go without reason, heedless of the real cost."

They got on it, three extremely intelligent folk with remarkable access to information. They ran down the source of the drug and got its specifications, then worked to craft an inexpensive source. It wasn't perfect, but it would do. Desiree would remain in remission, and she was no longer anchored to this area. None of them were.

"I don't know how to thank you," Desiree said. "You know I'm just a spent whore."

"*Were*," Quiti and Roque said almost together. "We won't be using that term in the future," Quiti concluded.

"You're with us now," Roque said. "We'll take care of you."

"You don't owe me anything."

"We don't know our own destinies," Quiti said. "Until the hairballs get back in touch and tell us what they want, we're on standby. At least we can help you with your situation. We know you and like you; that's enough."

Now it was Desiree's turn to weep. She had been reprieved from horror a second time.

"They're good people," Tillo said.

"And so are you," Desiree said, chastely hugging him.

They discussed options, and traveled, taking a flight to Gena's home where Desiree might have an adult companion who wouldn't judge her. They didn't even need to influence any minds; they simply earned enough money to cover the tickets for four.

Gena wasn't there, as Quiti had known from checking with her mentally. She would return the next day. They were welcome to use her house. Instead they found her daughter Idola, now 10, her prettiness verging on early beauty. She was minding the house, collecting the mail, sweeping the floors, and watering the plants. She was a responsible girl whose adoptive family gave her the leeway she deserved.

Idola welcomed Quiti like the friend she was. Then Quiti introduced Roque as her husband. "You're another hair suit!" the girl exclaimed. She picked up on that instantly; she had become attuned with Quiti.

"It seemed we were meant for each other," Roque said, glancing fondly at Quiti.

"That's so sweet."

Then the boy. "This is Tillo, whom we have adopted."

"You're a hair suit too!" Idola exclaimed. "Can you teach me telepathy?"

Tillo was at a loss for words, hating to disappoint this lovely girl his own age, but knowing that she lacked the capacity for telepathy despite her ability to sense it.

"Oh, I know," Idola said. "I'm not a hair suit. But maybe if I stick close to you, some of it'll rub off on me. I can feel your minds when they read mine."

"Maybe," Tillo said weakly. Quiti knew from his mind

that no girl of any age had ever found him interesting for any reason, and the idea of associating with this one excited him.

"Come on. I'll introduce you to my folks." Idola grabbed Tillo's hand and led him out of the house and toward her own, which was not far. He went quite willingly, and Quiti and Roque followed, bemused by this development.

Her family was working in their back yard. "Auntie Quiti's back!" Idola called. "And she's married! And they adopted a son my age!"

The parents took it in stride like the tolerant folk they were.

"Here's Tillo," Idola said. "He's my new boyfriend."

Quiti froze, caught by surprise by this additional aspect.

"You're too young," her mother said, smiling.

"Well, I'm adopted. He's adopted. So I adopted him as my boyfriend." She turned and kissed Tillo in a decidedly romantic fashion; he was similarly frozen.

"Idola, you hardly know him!"

"Sure I do." But now the girl paused, remembering that she couldn't tell anyone else about the hair suits, which was the real basis for her attraction.

Quiti thought fast. *Bring her butterflies,* she thought to the boy. *But not to eat.*

Tillo raised one hand and summoned butterflies. They flocked to him, many kinds, landing on the hand. Then they moved across to Idola, perching on her lifted hand and on her head, decorating her hair. It was an impressive and delightful little show.

Her mother threw up her hands, knowing how her daughter could be, and having more than a hint of how her daughter's friends could be. Then butterflies came to her too. The adoption logic might be strained, but it was allowed to stand. The gift of butterflies was a gesture that could not be denied. Idola had a boyfriend.

The upshot was that instead of parking Desiree at

Gena's house, they parked Tillo. Instead of taking Tillo to Quiti's neighborhood, they took Desiree.

"But be on guard," Quiti told Tillo as they parted. "There's an ambush in the making. We don't know exactly where it will strike; it could be here."

"I'll be alert," he agreed, more interested in having a real live girlfriend than in the follies of the authorities.

Speedo was waiting for them, having been alerted by Quiti's thought. Then he met Desiree. She was 21, close to the age Quiti had been when they were close, and attractive. He was now 18, of age. He hesitated, evidently fascinated.

"Yes, you may kiss her," Quiti said, laughing.

Speedo didn't laugh. He kissed Desiree, and the contact was sexually charged. She was shaken by the gesture, as Tillo had been with Idola, but hardly averse. She had not touched a man since entering the government program, because of the AIDS and her desire to go straight. Speedo was a handsome and virile young man who knew and liked Quiti as Desiree did; they had that in common. The sudden ramifications of this encounter were another surprise.

But it made a certain sense. Speedo knew that Quiti was now married, so was off the table, even if she did grant him one sexual event per her promise. Desiree could take or leave sex, but was highly competent at it. If she wanted to do it for fun instead of money, why not? Yet she hesitated because of her condition. She didn't want to expose another man to AIDS.

*You're in remission*, Quiti thought to her, amused. *Not infectious.*

"Let's get to know each other," Desiree said to Speedo. "There are things about me you may want to know."

"Yes," he agreed enthusiastically. Whether that attitude would remain once he learned Desiree's history would simply have to be seen. Probably it would.

"Be careful. We may be about to walk into an ambush,

and it could affect you."

Both Speedo and Desiree laughed. "Those ambushers don't know what they're getting into," Desiree said, and Speedo nodded. They smiled at each other, sharing the secret. Trying to ambush hair suits was an exercise in folly.

Quiti left the two of them to get to know each other better while she took Roque to meet her family. Even the limited amount she could afford to tell her parents was likely to shake them, but they would see that she had found a worthy man.

"This is where the trap is baited," Roque said, reading the ambiance.

"Then let's spring it. It's time."

As they approached the house, a man appeared wielding a cell phone. Quiti touched his mind. He was a spy, set to catch her if she ever showed up again. They still wanted her, as if there had ever been doubt. The police would be here in minutes.

She turned to Roque. "We have a choice," she said, repeating a dialogue they had rehearsed. "We can fade out, collect Desiree, and get the hell out of Dodge City. Or we can tough it out with the locals and make our stand."

"We can't let them confine us," he said. "We still have to find the hairballs."

"So we do." Then she did a double take, departing from the script. "The hairballs—I know where they are!"

"Where? Why haven't they shown up, since they promised that we'd see them again?"

"They've been with us all along. We're wearing them." She touched her hair.

"You're right," he said, amazed, touching his own hair. "They seeded us with their essence, and now they are part of us."

*Isn't that right?* she thought at her hair.

*It is right*, the hair agreed. *The original seeders are gone, as they could not endure long without proper hosts, but their spirits are with us, and you. We are hybrids.*

"What do you want of us?" she asked aloud.

*To be our ambassadors on Earth. To represent our interests before your people, so that we may exchange ideas and technology on an equal basis.*

"You want us to set up an alien embassy? A place considered part of your planet, sacrosanct, that will not be intruded upon?"

*Yes.*

"That would require a formal building, and a staff to operate its offices, diplomatic relations with the several nations of Earth. A big project."

*Yes.*

"And of course we'll do it."

"We already have several staff members lined up," Roque said. "Your friend Gena, and maybe her daughter Idola. Also Desiree and Speedo. I think they'll be glad to serve."

But Quiti had one more question for the hair. She had learned to look gift horses in the mouth. "Why did you choose us?"

*Four qualities of character, in ascending order of importance: Need, Tolerance, Compassion, Constancy.*

She reviewed those in her mind. The three of them had been in dire need at the time of encountering the hairballs, so that checked, and the hairballs had delivered in spades. Tolerance? None of them had been repulsed by the appearance of the aliens, accepting their right to be as they were. Compassion? All of them had tried to help the creatures, who seemed to be in distress, not knowing that no help was needed. But constancy? Their lives had changed wildly, as had their relationships. Everything had shifted, and the future remained uncertain. That did not seem to fit.

*We wish to establish diplomatic relations with the human kind on an equal basis. To do that we must win human respect, which in turn means showing equivalent power. But most humans are not emotionally equipped to handle power. Money is power to an extent. Poor humans who gain windfall riches are poor again within five years in more than nine of ten cases. Political power is more durable, but tends to corrupt, leading to mischief for both those who wield it and those who are wielded by it, as myriad dictatorships demonstrate. We need representatives who will not be corrupted by their power. Those were difficult to find.*

Quiti saw the sense if it. The three of them had never sought power or expected it, but they remained decent people despite acquiring powers unknown to their kind before. The aliens had chosen shrewdly.

But there was not time to ponder these revelations at the moment. A siren was approaching. "First there may be some pyrotechnics, as we demonstrate that we are not to be trifled with," Quiti said grimly. "We may have to show our powers openly."

"We are ready," Roque agreed. "We'll try to avoid violence."

Quiti hoped that was really the case. Much depended on the nature of the opposition they would face. Pacifism was not always effective.

They walked toward the house. The door opened and Quiti's mother appeared. "Quiti! Get away! It's a trap!"

Quiti was about to say that they knew it, but paused, realizing that it was more than they had anticipated. Suddenly they knew from Speedo and Desiree's minds, to which they had remained attuned in the background, that they were in trouble. What appeared to be a swat team was coming for them. At the same time, another team was going after Tillo in the other city. This was an elaborate sweep, exquisitely coordinated, preventing them from helping their friends. They were not just going after Quiti, Roque, and Tillo; they were taking their friends too, as hostages against any possible resistance.

"The idiots are getting smarter," Roque murmured. "They're playing dirty."

"I'll advise the others," Quiti said. "You work on this team."

She sent a thought to both Speedo and Desiree: *The trap is sprung. Stay put. Do not resist. Merely question them. Stall. We'll be there soon.*

*Got it,* Speedo replied.

Then she tuned to Tillo. *Do the unexpected. Summon animals, but don't attack unless you have to. Merely distract. Stall them. We'll handle the main thrust here.*

*I'm on it.*

Then she waited while Roque tuned to the squad coming after them. It was no longer necessary to catch a person's eye, but it did facilitate the implanting of illusions. During this pause she followed Tillo's situation as if standing behind him.

He was with Gena and Idola. "Do not move," he told them. They, knowing his nature, obeyed. He was new to them, but they knew him through Quiti: a hair suit.

The swat team came to stand before them. Five tough looking men. "We're taking you in, the three of you," the team leader said. "It will be better if you don't try to resist."

"We wouldn't think of it," Tillo said. "We're just a woman and two children here." However, the team had no idea what they were up against. They would soon learn. "But what about the animals?"

"The what?"

"The birds. The insects. The snakes."

The team members looked around. Wrens, robins, hawks, and an eagle were perching on nearby trees and shrubbery, and other birds were flying in. Several snakes were slithering close, some poisonous. A thick cloud of mosquitoes was forming.

"The pets," Tillo added.

Now dogs, cats, a potbellied pig, and several sheep were coming in. The animals formed a wide circle around the team.

"What gives?" the leader asked, realizing that something odd was occurring.

"They won't attack unless you do," Tillo said. "Fair is fair."

The leader took an angry step toward him. The circle of animals abruptly constricted, and all the creatures focused on the team, their eyes almost glowing. The mosquito cloud hovered closer, ferociously dense, now abetted by a swarm of bees. They were plainly ready to move in.

"Those mosquitoes look pretty hungry," Tillo remarked.

They did indeed. The men were armed and armored, but they were not prepared for this particular threat. Idola tittered.

"We have a situation," the leader said into his personal mike.

It was a standoff. It would hold for a while. Quiti had to return her attention to her own situation.

The swat team stood before them. "You're under arrest," the leader said.

"Whatever for?" Quiti inquired innocently, putting on her teen girl look with an accidental flash of cleavage.

"Disrupting the peace."

She frowned cutely and the flash deepened. "We wouldn't think of doing a horrible thing like that."

"Well then." The leader relaxed marginally, but the mission had not changed.

*Do the unexpected*, she thought to Roque.

*Statue of Liberty*, he agreed.

They went into action, mentally coordinated. Quiti's form appeared to change. She became a human sized Statue of Liberty, the 150 foot tall figure reduced to five and a half feet without sacrificing any grandeur, complete with spiked crown, tablet, and torch, her body more shapely than the original. Roque became Adonis, enhanced by musculature that would have done any comic book superhero credit. Both wore seeming capes that swung back to reveal their beautifully naked bodies.

The team members stared, and not just because of the seeming magic of the remarkable transformations. Quiti's natural figure was enough to stun the average man at ten feet, and these testosterone charged men were by no means average. Apart from her potent physical endowments, her torch actually seemed to be burning. But mainly, how could they arrest the Statue of Liberty, the ultimate symbol of American values? *Give me your tired, your poor, your huddled masses yearning to breathe free…* The statue was conceived as a gesture of international friendship, and became a world symbol of freedom. How could that symbol be abused?

But the swat team had a job to do, and would not be halted long by such a vision.

*The unexpected.*

Liberty and Adonis opened their mouths and sang, loudly, clearly, and passionately:

Mine eyes have seen the glory of the coming of the Lord:

He is trampling out the vintage where the grapes of wrath are stored;

He has loosed the fateful lightning of his terrible swift sword,

His truth is marching on.

At the reference to the sword, a bolt of lightning seemed to flash from it, and bright sparks radiated from the points of Liberty's crown as her torch flared. It was the "Battle Hymn of the Republic," the words by Julia Ward Howe, feelingly sung, soprano and tenor.

The swat team members stared. Then the leader stepped forward, turned smartly to face the others, lifted his arms, and conducted them as they broke into song, joining Liberty and Adonis.

Glory, glory hallelujah!
Glory, glory hallelujah!
Glory, glory hallelujah!
His truth is marching on.

Now the neighbors were coming out, amazed by the performance, along with Quiti's parents. They joined the chorus and fell in behind the swat team, which had become an honor guard.

Quiti and Roque turned in place and marched down the street, singing the second stanza. The swat team followed, singing and marching in step. The neighbors joined in behind, singing and marching. They all seemed to remember the words, culled from the common mindset.

A news helicopter appeared, having spied the activity. What was going on?

They came to where Speedo, Desiree, and their escort waited. Those folk smoothly joined the ensemble and the song.

They continued along the street, preempting traffic, singing one stanza after another. Folk poured out from every house and building to join the throng. It had become a patriotic parade. More copters appeared, tracking the impromptu spectacle.

They came at last to the city hall in the center of town. The crowd spread out, surrounding it, now thousands strong. The mayor and his staff emerged, thinking it was some kind of demonstration. He was correct, but he had underestimated its power. The song surrounded him.

In the beauty of the lilies Christ was borne across the sea,

With a glory in his bosom that transfigures you and me;

As he died to make men holy, let us die to make men free,

While God is marching on.


After the final refrain, they halted both the march and the song. The crowd stood, silent at last.

"And to what do we owe the honor of this remarkable serenade?" the mayor asked, not one to be daunted by a demonstration.

"We have come to establish an Embassy representing the alien Hair Brains," Quiti said, reverting to her natural form, modestly surrounded by her cloak of hair. "We need to appropriate your city hall as a temporary site until the formal one can be authorized and constructed."

The helicopters were hovering, recording the event for all the world to see, live. Reporters were making notes for phenomenal news stories. It was a highly public moment.

"Of course," the mayor said. He knew which way the wind was blowing. He was also conscious of the immense positive impact of the first alien world embassy, set up in this town. The local recession would be vaporized, and this region would become the center of global attention. Even a hoax would be great publicity.

The throng cheered. That included the swat teams. If any of their members realized that their thoughts had been subtly adjusted, they did not care to advertise it.

There remained formidable details to put in place, but Quiti knew that the corner had been turned. The authorities would not again try to interfere with this particular new order. Detente with the hair brains would be established. She looked forward to learning more about them.

*We chose well*, Quiti's hair thought.

"Yes you did," she agreed without false modesty, and Roque nodded.

They had an Embassy to organize.

Hallelujah!

# Author's Note

On August 6, 2015, I turned 81. That seemed like a fair accomplishment, because the average American man is several years dead by that age. On the 8th I made out with my wife, gratified that I was still capable of it. We've been married 59 years and will make 60 if death does not us part. On the 9th we had a visit from my collaborator on *Virtue Inverted*, Kenneth Kelly; that one's about a boy's adventures traveling with two tough men, and his relationship with a truly lovely and nice vampire girl, Virtue. On the 10th I had major dental surgery, with 11 teeth removed and 7 implants put in; with luck, that should end my chronic dental problems, as tooth implants don't decay. They are expensive; I will be most annoyed if I don't get at least a decade's use out of them, so I don't want to die too soon. Meanwhile I'm on the dread soft diet, unable to chew because I have no upper teeth. It's a nuisance, but part of what it takes to get my mouth in order.

On August 13th I started writing *Hair Power*, using its then working title *Hair Skirt*, which I felt was less relevant and maybe too suggestive. The idea came to me April 6, 2015, and again a month later, and I summarized it for my Ideas file: a woman with hair so long and voluminous that she could wear it in lieu of clothing, and it would keep her warm or cool, and when she whirled it would rise like a skirt to show as much of her body as she chose. I always liked long hair on a woman, so this is sort of my ultimate fantasy. Then of course I wondered how she came by it, and how it might affect her life. Might it have other properties, such as protecting her from attack, or facilitating the performance of her mind and body? Could it assist her swimming? Might it enable her to parachute, or even to fly? Could it emulate her normal clothing, so others would not notice it? How did she come by it? Could it be alien? So the idea grew somewhat as the hair grew, and you have seen the end result.

I don't think there's a connection, but while I was writing it, the global stock markets crashed, with back to back 500 point drops in the DOW, as there was concern about the economic situation of China.

But there was another concern. I read that some people have suffered memory loss or even general brain dysfunction when subjected to general anesthesia, particularly old folk. I'm old, so this put me at risk. I did not want to exchange bad teeth for bad memory. For one thing, it would mess up my writing. I've always said that if I should ever lose my writing ability, I would want to be the first, not the last, to know it. I have seen folk who claimed they were just as good in their age, or even better than ever. Like as not, they were in denial about their deterioration, substituting certainly for judgment. That can be dangerous when they happened to be in positions of responsibility or power, or driving a car. We have seen more than enough idiocy in high places. It's not a path I want to travel.

But how can I know, when my subjectivity will try to compensate for my decline? I exercise for my health, and my runs have slowed; those are measurable. But my thoughts? Sometimes I can tell, such as when I couldn't think of a certain type of food, and had to tell my wife it was round and we put mushrooms on it, and she said "Pizza." Right. I know the words, but can't always pull them out of my memory banks. There are more of those lapses as I age. If I get to the point of starting a story with "Once upon a ..." and can't think of the next word, I'll be concerned. But I'll probably dismiss it as a fluke, though that may not be the case.

So the timing of this novella was not coincidental. I scheduled it for right after my anesthesia in significant part to test my mental ability, trying to ascertain whether my writing finesse has suffered. It moved along okay; I wrote it in two weeks. But velocity is not the point; quality is. I think it is up to my normal standard, but I'm not sure. That will be up to you, my readers, to decide. I don't mean my critics, who seem to think that my brain had atrophied before I wrote and published my first word, over half a century ago. I mean my readers, who have liked my work in the past, but may find it lacking verve in the future. The thought of losing you is a horror, especially if it is because of my own failure.

Will there be a sequel? I have done many, many sequels elsewhere, and can take them or leave them. Obviously we have here a cast of characters with unusual powers and an important mission. I am curious about the culture and technology of Planet Hairball. But it depends less on them than on you, the readers: if this story is a success, there can be more. If not, not.

So that's it, my concern for the day. This novella was proofread by Scott M Ryan and Anne White. My website is www.hipiers.com/, where I have a monthly personal column, information on my novels, and maintain an ongoing survey of electronic publishers with candid feedback from authors who use them. The idea is to help others get a less difficult start than I did, before I grew my hair long. So if you want to know more about me, that's where to go. Otherwise, I'm glad you read this book, and hope, oh do I hope, you enjoyed it.

# ABOUT THE AUTHOR

Piers Anthony is one of the world's most prolific and popular authors. His fantasy Xanth novels have been read and loved by millions of readers around the world, and have been on the *New York Times* Best Seller list many times. Although Piers is mostly known for fantasy and science fiction, he has written several novels in other genres as well, including historical fiction, martial arts, and horror. Piers lives with his wife of 60 years in a secluded woods hidden deep in Central Florida.

Piers Anthony's official website is HI PIERS at www.hipiers.com, where he publishes his monthly online newsletter. HI PIERS also has a section reviewing many of the online publishers and self-publishing companies for your reference if you are looking for a non-traditional solution to publish your book.

Made in the USA
San Bernardino, CA
03 January 2018